The Night Branders

The Night Branders

WALT COBURN

Library of Congress Cataloging-in-Publication Data

Coburn, Walt, 1889-1971.
The night branders / Walt Coburn.
p. cm.
ISBN 1-57490-517-1 (alk. paper)
1. Americans—Mexico—Fiction. 2. Fathers—Death—Fiction.
3. Cattle theft—Fiction. 4. Revenge—Fiction. 5. Mexico—Fiction. 6. Large type books. I. Title.
PS3505.O153N54 2003
813'.52—dc22 2003020414

Cataloging in Publication Data is available from the British Library and the National Library of Australia.

Sagebrush Large Print Westerns are published in the United States and Canada by Thomas T. Beeler, Publisher, PO Box 659, Hampton Falls, New Hampshire 03844-0659. ISBN 1-57490-517-1

Published in the United Kingdom, Eire, and the Republic of South Africa by Isis Publishing Ltd, 7 Centremead, Osney Mead, Oxford OX2 0ES England. ISBN 0-7531-6928-2

Published in Australia and New Zealand by Bolinda Publishing Pty Ltd, 17 Mohr Street, Tullamarine, Victoria, Australia, 3043 ISBN 1-74030-935-9

Manufactured by Sheridan Books in Chelsea, Michigan.

The Night Branders

CAST OF CHARACTERS

TOM STROUD

Secretly he sought his kinfolk's murderer. Was that man seeking *him?*

IKE BABCOCK

He was as amiable and soft-spoken as they came—until he decided a man was his enemy.

COLONEL RUIZ

His favorite music at a *baile* was the rat-tat-tat of the firing squad and the thud of his prisoners' falling bodies.

KID BRADY

This gunslick could do more on a bottle of red sody pop than most could do on a gallon of firewater.

KING KENNEDY

A monarch whose subjects were herds of rustled cattle, and whose scepter was a smoking .45!

LUTHER JOHNS

He dealt in everything: hairpins, wetback cattle, and other men's lives.

BORDER RENEGADES

THE DAY BEFORE, a trail herd of wet cattle had come up out of somewhere in Mexico. The outfit had camped on the banks of Cayuse Creek. A dozen or more bearded men, all armed, all branded with that mark that is worn by the border renegade, they had painted the squalid little cow town of Cayuse a crimson hue. All night those renegade cowboys drank and sang and quarreled and played poker. At daylight they had pulled out, leaving a dead man in the back room of the town's one saloon. The dead man had *been* one of them. The killing was the outcome of an old grudge, brought to life by bad whisky.

The cattle drive had gone on. The dead man was buried, with little ceremony, without even a coffin, in a grave at the edge of town. In a few days or weeks the drifting sand would hide the mark of the grave, even as it had hidden other graves. The town of Cayuse, just north of the Mexican border, paid little attention to shooting scrapes. Located on the mesquite and cactus-spotted desert near the foot of the Red Mountains, it knew no law save the law of a six-gun —and the law of Luther Johns.

Luther Johns, owner of the Cayuse Trading Post, dealer in everything from hairpins to wet cattle.

More than one stranger, upon seeing Luther Johns, had likened the man to a human buzzard. He was long of arm and leg, skinny, with a bald head, hawk nose, and a thin slit of a mouth. His right eye was a bloodshot greenish slit. On the other side of the bony ridge of a nose was a terribly scarred, eyeless socket.

A cloth patch would have hidden the revolting scar, but it was typical of Luther Johns that he preferred to let the maimed eye socket remain uncovered. He took a grisly delight in watching men and women shudder as they looked at him. He might have been forty—or seventy.

The Cayuse storekeeper had long-fingered hands with dirty, uncut nails. His linen was never clean, and his black broadcloth coat and trousers were spotted, greenish. The only things clean about the man were the two pearl-handled six-guns he carried, and the sawed-off shotgun behind the littered counter. A counter piled with blankets, tarps, latigo straps, saddle cinches, hard twist rope, tobacco, bales of bright calico, bolts of ribbon, and all manner of odds and ends.

At the rear of the store was a big safe. Once upon a time the safe had been in a Tombstone gambling house. The name of the original owner was still on it, in gilt letters.

At the end of the counter was a cot, a makeshift cot covered with smelly, unclean blankets. Here it was that Luther Johns did his sleeping—a few hours at night, an afternoon siesta.

It was past the noon hour now. Luther Johns's one eye was red-rimmed. He had not slept for forty-eight hours. He closed his big safe and unbuckled his gun belt. He dropped the belt and holstered guns down alongside the cot. Then he removed his shabby boots. He sat on the edge of the bunk and rolled himself a cigarette which was a mixture of tobacco and *marijuana.* The same tobacco he sold to those who craved drugged smoking. He sat there on his cot, running over in ins mind the profits he had made since that drive had come across the border.

There was his commission on the twenty-five thousand cash which he now held in his safe until delivery of the cattle had been verified by the Cross X outfit. There were the profits he had made from the saloon and gambling tables which he controlled. A hundred dollars for planting that renegade cowboy who had fought over a Mexican girl at the cantina which belonged to him. All of it safe money.

Only fools took chances and risked their lives and liberty. Fools like "King" Kennedy, who owned the Cross X, and Jack Jackson and "Kid" Brady. Jackson and Kid Brady were King Kennedy's gunmen. King took an occasional chance, when he was drunk or on the prod. Jackson, better known as Jack, or the "Jack of Spades," took chances when his trigger finger got itchy. Kid Brady, hardly out of his teens, wouldn't last long with his marked cards, his hot temper, and his spitting gun. Fools. Fools.

It was a hot afternoon. Heat waves made the horizon a distorted, unreal outline, ever changing. Luther Johns finished his cigarette and stretched out on his cot. He was tired, tired in every muscle and nerve. He'd take his siesta. The front door was locked. He remembered that he had bolted it. The *tequila* he had been drinking for forty-eight hours was taking its toll. The smoke made him sleepy. He lay back on his unclean blankets, his head on a pillow that had long ago lost all semblance of whiteness. On his back, mouth open, he slept.

He woke with a start. When he reached for his guns, a strong, brown hand shoved him back. He saw a man in jumper and overalls, his lower face, from the eyes down, covered by a black silk bandana.

"The siesta hour," said a drawling voice, "is about up for you. Hate to bust up yore snoring', but we got some business to take care of. Kinda private, you might say. Git up an' open that safe. Make a bad move and you'll go where they been waitin' for you a long time."

Slowly, his one bloodshot eye glittering, Luther Johns got to his feet. His lipless mouth twitched. He reached for the bottle of *tequila* on the floor beside his bunk. His guns were gone. A pair of eyes, cold as the gray of a winter sky, watched him. There was a wry grin hidden behind the scarf that served as a mask.

"Shaky, Mr. Man?" drawled the other's voice. "You better take a good slug o' that *tequila.* Then open the safe."

"You're either drunk or loco, whoever you are. You can't get twenty miles from here without being killed."

"I'm riskin' that, buzzard. Open up, or I'll git ornery. Open that safe!"

Luther Johns sat in the back room of the saloon. Facing him were three men. King Kennedy was a big, florid man, with a heavy paunch and sharp, whitish eyes set in a fowled face that was lined by broken little veins. The face of a man who had lived hard—a man who had ridden hard, fought hard, and drank whisky as most men drink water. King Kennedy, owner of the Cross X. King Kennedy, whose men crossed the border in spite of all patrol officers.

Next to him sat Jackson. The Jack of Spades. Black-eyed, lean-faced, and black-haired. A silent-lipped man who sipped raw whisky from a water glass.

Next to Jack Jackson sat a young cowboy barely out of his teens. He had light blue eyes, a sallow face, and hair the color of new rope. His nose was blunt, wide of nostril. His mouth was wide, and when he grinned, which was a lot of time, his bared lips showed a set of strong, large, irregular, yellowish teeth. He wore his six-gun tied low on his thigh. His hands were long-fingered, deft, the hands of a gambler. This was Kid Brady, with a killer's record that was appalling. And he was as handy with a cold deck or a pair of crooked dice as he was with his .45. He was the personal bodyguard of King Kennedy. He drank red soda pop from the bottle and chewed gum.

Luther Johns faced the three men. His one greenish eye glittered like the eye of a snake.

"The money's gone, King, and that's all there is to it."

"You wouldn't be fool enough to double-cross me, would you, Luther?" asked Kennedy, leaning across the table.

"No," came the curt reply.

King Kennedy nodded as if satisfied by the brief monosyllable. His eyes, strangely faded against the red-brown face, stared unblinkingly at Luther Johns.

"What did he look like?"

"Like any other cow-puncher. Overalls, boots, and a hat that had seen better days."

"How about his spurs? Spur straps?"

"He'd taken off his spurs. He had gray eyes and sandy hair. The rest of his face was covered."

"What did his voice sound like?"

"Like Jackson's," replied Luther Johns, lighting his cigarette.

Jack Jackson's thin lips twisted. "Meanin' what, yuh one-eyed buzzard?"

"Meaning," said Luther Johns in that voice of his which was like a rasping croak, "that the man talked like a Texican. No need to get touchy, Jack. I said he had gray eyes. Yours are black. Tuck in your shirt, pardner."

Kid Brady grinned widely. He liked to see quarrels start. And none of these men wasted any love on one another. All of them worked for King Kennedy. And their loyalty to the big cattleman was paid for with money which they earned, each in his own way. There was a sort of jealousy between them. Jackson bore the brunt of the hard work. He handled the wet cattle that came up out of Mexico. Kid Brady traveled all over the country with King Kennedy, having a good time, staying at good hotels, eating the best of grub. Jackson's fare was mostly beans and jerky. His bed was wherever the outfit made camp.

As for Luther Johns, he stayed in Cayuse, drank his *tequila,* smoked his vile cigarettes, and handled the deals between King Kennedy and the men who brought stolen cattle out of Mexico. He was the "fence" for King Kennedy and the rustlers. Kennedy never dealt directly with them.

Seldom did King Kennedy ever see Jack Jackson. Jackson took the risks and was paid for it. King Kennedy spent most of his time around the border towns where he had gambling and saloon concessions. He had a stable of race horses which he followed from Agua Caliente to New Orleans. But the bulk of his money came from the Cross X Ranch.

"I didn't come clear from California to listen to you idiots argue," he growled, biting off the end of a fifty-cent cigar. "I come here to find out what's gumming the cards. I get a wire from Jackson saying the last bunch of cattle driven up and delivered was stampeded. Spilled. Nine-tenths of 'em back in Mexico. Then a wire from Luther saying he's been robbed of the money posted to pay for that drive of dogies. I hightail it here and have to listen to a lot of jabber. I want facts. I'll git facts or know the reason why. I met you here tonight to get at the bottom of this business. Jackson and his spilled herd. Luther and his robbed safe. There's somethin' wrong."

His heavy fist banged the table. Kid Brady grabbed his bottle of pop just in time. He grinned widely at Jackson and Luther Johns. He liked to watch them sweat under King Kennedy's questioning. Because he hated them both.

"Here," growled the big cattleman, "is the situation as I got it from the right sources: Two thousand head of cattle were delivered here at Cayuse. I'd contracted with Ike Babcock for that many head. Babcock counted the cattle over to Jackson, then took his men and drifted. He tells Luther to keep the money in the safe because he's goin down into the Yaqui country to pick up some more cattle and he don't want to pack that much money on him. It ain't the first time Ike Babcock had left money here. Luther, if you had half the money sense you should have you'd made him sign up for the money on delivery of the cattle. But he never even come to town. How do I know but what he ain't in on the deal? By rights it's Ike Babcock, not me, that's out the money. How about it, Luther?"

"The money ain't his till he signs the receipt. That's in the agreement you both signed. You hold the empty sack, King."

"All right. I'll mark it up to experience. Now we get back to what happened. Some of Babcock's men is left in town, drinkin' and gamblin' and so on. Most o' my outfit is in town, from what I hear. All of 'em lappin' up liquor. Four men on guard when that herd of snuffy steers busts loose and are spilled all over the country.

And nobody has any clear idea how they come to stampede. I'm out the best part o' two thousand head o' dogie steers that headed straight back to Mexico.

"Then some gent rides into town in broad daylight, sticks up Luther, and rides off with twenty-five thousand dollars o' my money. So I lose fifty thousand dollars because you two boneheads lay down on the job. Any other man 'ud kill you. But I'm lettin' you both off light. Jackson will work out his part of the loss. And Luther is goin' to dig down into his unwashed sock and pay Ike Babcock twenty-five thousand cash, less his percentage."

Jackson's hand gripped his tumbler full of raw whisky. His dark face was mask-like, but there was hatred and resentment in his black eyes. He had made money along the border and he knew that King Kennedy had always suspected him of getting money on the side. Perhaps Kennedy had proof. Ike Babcock might have talked some, in his drunken moments, about the private deals between him and Jack Jackson. He sipped his whisky and said nothing.

"Got it straight, Jackson?" growled Kennedy.

"Plenty."

"You got any holler comin', Luther?"

Luther Johns shook his head.

King Kennedy got to his feet. Kid Brady, grinning widely, hitched up his gun belt. He had hoped Jackson and Luther Johns would start something.

"We'll have a drink out at the bar," said King Kennedy, brushing his shirt. His coat and trousers were of good material, tailored to fit his huge frame. He paid real money for the shirts he had made to fit him. His boots came from the oldest boot maker in Texas. His hat, a gray, wide-brimmed, high-crowned Stetson, was of the best beaver. Under his left armpit he carried a big .45 automatic. Only Kid Brady knew of the smaller gun that the big cattleman carried in a specially made pocket inside the waistband of his trousers.

"Everybody satisfied?" he asked, grinning faintly. "No beefing? Jack? Luther?"

"We'll take what we got comin'," said Jackson.

"One thing, before we go out there into the saloon. Who was that cowboy that got killed? One of our boys?"

Luther Johns's one eye looked at Jackson. It winked swiftly. King Kennedy, who was looking at Jackson, missed the signal. But Kid Brady saw it and grinned faintly.

"Dunno what was his name, King," replied Jackson. "He was one of our cowboys. A young gent about the age o' Kid Brady. He asked for what he got."

"Who killed him?" asked Kennedy, as he let Luther Johns and Jackson pass out the door.

"I killed him," Jackson called back across his shoulder.

IKE BABCOCK

"GIT WORD TO IKE Babcock," said King Kennedy, as they stood at the bar, "that I want more cattle. Two thousand head of wet cattle under the same agreement."

"I'll let 'im know," said Jackson grimly.

Even as they spoke, a tall, raw-boned, bronzed, unshaven man came into the place. He wore chaps that were service-scarred. His brush jumper was shabby, torn at one shoulder. His puckered, hazel eyes, half-brown, half-gray in color, looked at the men at the bar.

The others looked at him and nodded. He was over six feet tall, and his bones were large, his joints knotty. His face was roughly hewn, homely. There was a humorous grin on his wide mouth.

"How are yuh, Babcock?" King Kennedy held out a thick hand which was gripped in the brush-scarred, bony hand of Ike Babcock.

"Doin' so-so, Kennedy. Howdy, Jackson. H're you, Luther? I just got word about the bad luck Luther had. Left the boys workin' down yonder and come on up."

"Afraid you'd lose yore money?" asked King Kennedy.

"Nope. I ain't worryin'."

"The money was taken," said Luther Johns, "after delivery of the cattle. By rights, Ike, it was your money that was grabbed."

"Then let it go at that," said the raw-boned rustler. "If that's the way you boys do business, let 'er go at that. Looks like the drinks are on me."

"Luther," said King Kennedy, giving the storekeeper a swift, sharp look, "has his own idea about jokes. You git yore money, Ike, the same as always. Luther Johns bought the cattle and he'll pay for 'em. Then he sold the cattle to me. The same as always."

Ike Babcock shrugged his wide shoulders and reached for tobacco and papers.

"Whatever you boys say always goes with me. Got a match, Jackson? Thanks. Heard you spilled the cattle?"

"You been hearin' a lot, ain't you?" replied Jackson.

"News travels."

"And cattle drift." Kennedy chuckled. "I bet you've gathered up two-thirds o' that spilled herd, already. Them Mexican dogies is home-lovin' critters. Bet a hat you've gathered the bulk of 'em, down below. Do I win or lose?"

"Meanin' a hat or them dogies?" The lanky cowpuncher grinned.

"I've done lost the dogies. I'm bettin' a new hat that you've gathered most o' that herd that stampeded south."

Ike Babcock's homely grin widened. He lifted his battered hat and scratched his uncut, uncombed mop of reddish hair.

"Dunno, King. Mexican cattle looks alike, and them Figger Curious brands is harder to read than Chinee. We done gathered some cattle the last few days, to be sure. I figgered you'd want some. I'll give you the benefit o' the doubt, even if I don't know the names o' the cattle that got strayed off. When you git to Phoenix, pick out yore hat." And he winked broadly at Kid Brady.

Kid Brady grinned back. He had once worked for Ike Babcock. Wrangled horses and punched cows for him. He liked to hear the big, good-natured cowman laugh. As some cowboy had once said of him, "Ike Babcock uses his whole face when he laughs."

He laughed now. Kennedy's florid face broke in a grin. But neither Jackson nor the one-eyed Luther Johns were in any mood for smiling. Each had booked a loss.

"I'll have you another bunch o' dogies in two weeks. How many will you want, King?"

"Luther buys the cattle," the wily Kennedy reminded him. "You do business with Luther. I never bought so much as a wind-bellied calf from you in my life. I buy cattle from Luther Johns, the cattle buyer of Cayuse."

Ike Babcock nodded. "How many, Luther?"

"Two thousand head. Twelve fifty a head, delivered here at Cayuse. No culls."

"I don't handle culls. When I fetch cattle here, they're

good cattle and in good shape, considerin'. A little spooky, mebbe, but then a man can't find milk-pen stuff down in the rough country. By the time they reach here, they're gentle enough. But you ain't buyin' this next bunch for any twelve and a half. They'll cost you fifteen dollars."

Luther Johns looked at King Kennedy. The florid-faced cattleman stared hard at Ike Babcock.

"Fifteen is too much, I'd say," said Kennedy, looking now at Luther Johns. "Thirteen is as high as you can go, Luther."

"Then there won't be any cattle delivered here, gents. Fifteen is my price. I kin git it from other buyers. Even then I'm not makin' much. And I'm takin' big risks."

Luther Johns snorted. "You aren't talking to a kindergarten class, Babcock. Your men get about two or three dollars a head for what they gather. Crossing the border is no trouble for a man who understands the game. The bulk of the cattle you'll deliver will be from the herd that Jackson spilled when—"

A low snarl from Jackson. "I've heard enough about that herd spilling. That goes for all of you. I'm payin' through the nose, but I ain't goin' to have it throwed in my teeth by you, Johns, or any other man."

"Quit this fool janglin'," growled King Kennedy. "Jackson, nobody is mentioning that herd again. Luther, don't let us interrupt yore dicker with Ike."

"Thirteen is my top price, Babcock."

"Whatever you say goes, Luther. There's other markets. No hard feelin's."

"Not that I want to be hornin' in," said Kennedy, puffing his cigar, "but what's the idea in raisin' the ante, Ike?"

"It's goin' to he harder to make delivery. Cayuse

orter have a daily newspaper so that you boys could keep up with th' times. You ain't heard the latest?"

"Meanin' what?" asked Kennedy.

"Meanin', for one thing, that they've doubled the border patrol. They're closin' up the gaps."

"That all?"

"Not all, no. I got word to quit handlin' my li'l ol' dogies. Whoever wrote the letter didn't sign it. He said he was warnin' me to quit dealin' with Luther because he was hangin' a few hides on the fence and because I'd done him a favor once, he didn't want to see my homely hide among the others."

"Who is he after?" asked Kennedy.

"Every man connected in any way with the Cayuse Cattle Pool."

The others looked at one another. Kennedy, Kid Brady, Jackson, Luther Johns exchanged glances. Kennedy, Jackson, and Johns were known as the "Cayuse Cattle Pool." Kid Brady was simply Kennedy's bodyguard.

"And you aim to let a fool letter like that bluff you out, do you, Babcock?" asked Kennedy.

"It might be my herd, not yourn, Kennedy, that will git spilled next time: Don't go gittin' on the prod, Jackson. But I had to explain my side. Somebody stampeded them cattle. It wasn't no natural run. And it wasn't no bluff when Luther's safe was robbed. The same gent might be layin' for me when I leave here tonight. The gent that wrote that letter is the man that stampeded Jackson's herd. The same man that robbed Luther's safe. And because he'll likely take a crack at my herd, I got to hire more men. And good men cost money. The gent that wrote that letter to me ain't runnin' any whizzer. He means what he says. Well, boys, I got to be driftin' down the trail. Fifteen is my price. Take it or leave it."

He set down his empty glass. His puckered hazel eyes looked at the others. He was grinning amiably.

Luther Johns looked at Kennedy. King Kennedy scowled and puffed his big cigar. He liked to drive a close bargain. But the tall, raw-boned Ike Babcock was a hard man to bargain with. When he named a price, it stood.

"Give him fifteen, Luther. Delivery in two weeks."

THE TALL STRANGER

IKE BABCOCK HAD RIDDEN out of town, pushing hard for the Mexican line. If ever there lived a fearless man, it was this homely, good-natured border cowboy who brought cattle out of Mexico. Most men in his dangerous position would have taken along at least one man as bodyguard. But Ike Babcock was not that way. He liked to ride alone. Now, with a small fortune in the pocket of his overalls, he rode with no thought of fear in his heart.

He grinned to himself as he recalled his meeting with those men in Cayuse. Contempt, rather than any hatred, marked his feelings toward Kennedy, Jackson, and Luther Johns. He knew them for what they were, and classed them among the coyotes, not the wolves. For Kid Brady he had a certain amount of friendship, though he knew that the young killer was by far the most dangerous man connected with the Cayuse Cattle Pool. He hoped he would never have to shoot it out with the Kid. He had a respect for the young killer's gun, to be sure, but he did not fear him. He knew that, if the time came when they would become enemies, Kid Brady would give him an even break. And if he did, it would be the Kid, not Ike Babcock, who would drop first. Because Ike Babcock was by far the faster man with a six-gun.

Ike Babcock would go to any lengths to avoid a quarrel with any man. He liked to laugh and he was forever playing rough jokes. And he would ride all night to attend a dance, be it a Mexican *baile* or an old-fashioned hoedown on this side of the line. And he danced with them all—young and old, the ugly and the beautiful. And never once did he miss a number.

He knew how to talk the sort of talk that the women liked. Mexican or American, he talked to them in their own language. Not love talk, for there was nothing of the lover about Ike Babcock. But he would know if a woman had on a new dress or was doing her hair differently. And he would have them laughing and chattering. From grandmothers to small children he knew how to make them laugh.

Even down in Mexico, where men feel differently about their women, they would postpone a fiesta or *baile* until Ike Babcock could get there and join them. Oftentimes he would be the only gringo there. No husband or lover was ever jealous of him. No father was ever afraid to trust his daughter with this big, laughing cowboy.

He rode hard tonight, covering the distance between Cayuse and the border. A twenty-mile ride. The big gelding under him was one of the best road horses ever bred. Gaunt of flank, game-hearted, tireless. Traveling at a long trot. Rough-gaited, but tough as rawhide.

He halted at a camp along the line. The camp was deserted. He unsaddled and hobbled his horse and made a fire. He made coffee and Dutch-oven biscuits and fried some meat. It was just breaking day.

The camp was a simple affair. A Dutch-oven spread, a one-man tepee that held the owner's bed. A brush corral.

The campfire glowed in the early dawn. The lanky cowboy sat cross-legged on the ground, eating hungrily, washing down the simple grub with black coffee. He did not even look around as two riders came up behind him.

"Well, I'm —" One of the riders swung off his horse.

Ike looked up at the man in jumper and chaps.

"I built enough biscuits for three," said Ike grinning. "What you gawkin' at, mister?"

The other rider, a gun in his hand, now joined his companion. They stared down at Ike Babcock, who was chewing placidly on his steak.

"Ain't you Ike Babcock?" asked the younger of the two men. Both wore badges pinned to their brush jumpers.

"You guessed right the first time. Hope you don't mind me kinda makin's myse'f at home."

The two men looked at each other. The older one smiled faintly.

"Not at all, Babcock. Matter of fact, we've been hunting all night for you. We've ridden our horses down trying to locate you."

"Somethin' important?"

The older man's lips tightened in a wry smile. He was a man in his fifties, square-built, a trifle paunchy.

"Nothing much, Babcock, only a big bunch of cattle were shoved across the border after dark last night. Mexican cattle. Wet cattle. We located the cattle and the men about twenty-five miles east of here, at the old Lazy P Ranch. None of the men would tell us who owned the cattle. They said they didn't know anything except that they were to hold the cattle there. They claimed they didn't even know the man they worked for. And they swore that the cattle had been gathered on the United States side of the line. How about it, Babcock?"

"If I was you boys," said Ike Babcock, "I'd take their word for anything they said."

"Meaning you're not talking?"

"Meanin'," said Ike Babcock, cleaning his plate with the last of his biscuit, "that when a man ain't got anything to say, he better keep his mouth shut. Unsaddle an' tie into this grub before it gits cold. And mister, you don't need a gun in yore hand to talk to Ike Babcock. You gents are new here along this part o' the border. New brooms sweep clean, as the sayin' goes, but a man better be plumb certain he's makin' the right motions with them brooms. Unsaddle an' take 'er easy."

"Not till we find out what you're doing here, Babcock." The eyes of the border patrol officer were menacing, cold.

"Me? I'm here eatin' breakfast. Just come from Cayuse. Found yore camp and made myse'f at home. If yo're the kind o' men that charge for camp grub, I'll—" Ike Babcock left the sentence unfinished as he pulled a thick roll of money from his pocket. He peeled off a hundred-dollar bill and laid it on his empty plate. Then he got to his feet. The plate with the money lay on the ground beside the campfire. He grinned at the two patrol riders.

"That orter pay for what I put away. I don't ever stay at any man's camp when I ain't as welcome as the flowers in May. I'll saddle my pony an' be on my way."

"Not so fast, Babcock. Where'd you get all that

money?"

"I keep the answers to them kind o' questions. I got quite a big-sized collection of 'em. They're on file at my lawyer's office. I been supportin' that slick-dressin', bald-headed li'l ol' shyster fer years. Ask him yore questions, mister. And put up that gun. I git kind o' nervous when a man holds a gun on me. Didn't they tell you boys about me when they sent you here?"

"They sent us here to wipe out this rustling. We're going to do it. Babcock, what do you know about those cattle?"

"I'll ask you one, mister. Did you read the brands on 'em? Did you read the fresh brand on every critter in that herd?"

"It was too dark. Too dark to read brands."

"Then you better take a ride over there this mornin'. You'll find Kennedy's Cross X brand on every critter them boys is holdin'." Ike Babcock grinned widely.

"Then they're Kennedy's cattle?"

"I said them dogies was in his iron. That usually makes 'em belong to the brand owner. No cattle was crossed last night by my outfit. Some gent has been jobbin' you boys. If I was you, I'd make plumb sure what I was doin' before I made ary long night rides. And before you make ary gun play, have a talk with some o' the old-timers around here."

Ike Babcock bridled and saddled his horse and shoved his carbine into its saddle scabbard. The two new patrol officers eyed him in silence. Now, as the lanky cowboy stepped aboard his horse, one of the men picked the hundred-dollar bill from the empty tin plate.

"You forgot this, Babcock."

"When I eat at a camp where I ain't welcome, I pay for my grub. That's the smallest I got on me. Leave the change with Luther Johns at Cayuse some day. My place is forty-fifty miles below the border. Come down an' see us work, some time. The meals is free to any man. So long." And he rode away, leaving them scowling after him.

The older one of the pair swore softly as he unsaddled. His younger companion's face was a little red.

"The next time you get a hot tip," growled the older law officer, "verify it. Somebody's tricked us. Most likely Ike Babcock put up the job on us. We can't touch those cattle, if they're in Kennedy's brand. And all we have against Babcock is that he ate breakfast and paid for it with a hundred-dollar bill. The joke's on us, and I don't like it."

Ike Babcock changed horses at a Mexican ranch that he used as a way station. He spent half an hour talking to the old Mexican, who looked after the string of grain-fed horses there.

"The boys went up with the whisky, Farias?" he asked the old man in the Mexican tongue.

"*Si señor,* and returned with the guns."

"*Bueno.* The trick worked this time. But it won't work a second time. One of those patrol officers is no pilgrim at the business. He won't be easy to fool again."

The old Mexican chuckled. "You will fool them many more times, Señor. But I almost forgot. A letter was left for you last night. Here."

Ike Babcock opened the unaddressed envelope. He read the brief contents of the note, then stuffed it into his pocket.

"Who left it, Farias? What did the man look like?"

"It was too dark to make him out, señor."

"Mexican?"

"No. An Americano."

Ike Babcock rode on to his ranch in the rough mountains. The letter in his pocket warned him to quit whisky smuggling and gun-running and to break with the Cayuse Cattle Pool.

Ike Babcock and Luther Johns controlled the liquor running and gun-running along this part of the border. Ike had sent the decoy message to the new patrol officers. The man who "tipped off" the patrol riders was a Mexican in the uniform of a federal officer of the army. The uniform was stolen. The man wearing it was one of Ike's several lieutenants. With the patrol officers gone, the pack train had gone up, laden with whisky and *tequila.* It had returned with guns to be sold to a Mexican bandit who had hopes of some day leading a revolution.

"They want whisky across the line," Ike argued, "and this feller down here wants guns. This is between me and you, Luther. Don't cut in King Kennedy or Jackson."

So they had worked together. The crafty Luther Johns, the hard-riding Ike Babcock. And they had made money. Ike's share went into his ranch in Mexico. More land, more cattle, more horses. He was spreading out. He was one of the biggest cattlemen in that section of Mexico. And to all appearances, the big, easy-grinning cowman thought it no crime to run guns and whisky.

But the two letters he had received worried him more than he would admit. If it was the law that was warning him, he was willing to lay low for a few months.

The officers along the border had always been fair to him. To them it was a game. Ike Babcock usually managed to outwit them. But now and then a pack train would be captured, or he would be forced to turn loose a bunch of cattle. That was all part of the game. When he met the border officers in town, they would josh one another. Now and then he would bet a hat or a horse or ten bucks that he'd pass the next pack train across without his men being caught and the contraband confiscated.

It was a game which Ike Babcock loved. Never once had he attempted to bribe one of them, and they respected and liked him for it. He stopped often at their camps. They were always welcome at his ranch. And on three occasions he had turned over to them men who were running dope.

He hated dope-runners. He fought them whenever the opportunity came up. He had also fetched out of Mexico a few murderers—a man who had murdered his wife for her jewels and money; another man who had waylaid and murdered a border patrol officer; and two others who had dry-gulched their victims.

Ike Babcock had no quarrel with the border officers. If the writer of those letters was one of them, he'd heed the advice.

But if it was some tough gent trying to bluff him into quitting the game, that was different. He'd show this letter-writing hombre that whenever any man undertook to push Ike Babcock aside, he had tackled a real job.

Ike reckoned he'd hunt up one or two of the old-timers among the border patrol men and find out what they knew. They'd tell him the truth. They wouldn't lie.

At the ranch he was given a boisterous welcome by his pack of hounds. He was hardly off his horse before they were upon him, pawing him, whining and yelping, licking his hands and face. Great Danes, Irish wolfhounds, greyhounds, staghounds; from the giant Danes and Irish wolfhounds down to the newest litter of waddling puppies that chewed at his chaps and threatened to trip him.

When he had turned loose his horse, he went to the house with the cowboy who had met him at the barn.

The ranch house was a rambling old adobe, rebuilt from the ruins of the original place. Time had been when the place had been owned by the padres. Ike had rebuilt the mission down below the ploughed ground that grew alfalfa and grain and grapes and fruit. Two Mexican families cared for the chapel. Now and then a traveling padre paid a visit, and Ike would send out word to all his men who wanted to come to Mass.

From the most lowly peon who worked in the fields, to the Mexican major-domo who handled his Mexican vaqueros, they worshipped this big renegade. They all had their own houses, their gardens, a few head of goats, a few burros. There were many fiestas here at the old ranch. Barbecues, dancing, music, cowboy contests. There was much rivalry between the Mexican vaqueros and the cowboys Ike brought down from north of the border. Now and then there would be a fight, but not often. Because Ike Babcock stood for no fighting among his men. If two men quarreled, they would either shake hands or draw their pay.

He went on to the house now, swinging along with jingling spurs. He greeted the bearded Mexican who had been sitting in the shade of the vine-covered arcade.

They shook hands, and a servant brought drinks. This was the Mexican bandit who bought guns and ammunition and dreamed of being at least a governor. He had a high, wide forehead, fine eyes, a firm mouth. He liked to visit here at the old ranch of the padres. He had been born here in this old adobe building. His father had been holder of a large grant, part of which Ike

Babcock now leased. The wine he now sipped had been made when he was a boy. He had shown Ike where the huge casks were hidden in a vault behind a false wall of the old granary.

They sat talking until suppertime. The bandit's men, save for his personal bodyguard, had gone with the guns to the rebel stronghold back in the mountains.

"I can't deliver any guns for a while," Ike told him. "Not until I find out who wrote me this letter. If it's one of the patrol boys, I'll lay off. But if it is one of that renegade pack north of the line, I'll keep on dealin'. I'm goin' to find out."

The bearded bandit nodded and twisted his heavy moustache. He understood.

"That is for you to decide, my good friend. Besides, I have not the money right now for more guns.

"Yore credit's always good, Colonel. It ain't that."

"Thees letter, eet make you worry, no? That ees too bad. You want to know what thees man look like who leave the letter weeth old Farias? I tell you. He ees a tall man weeth hair the color of buckskin. He has gray eyes. He talk like a Texas man. He stop at my camp. But I am not there at the time. He say he ees good frien' to you, but he does not geev hees name. Always, when a stranger ees come an' leave, my *hombrecitos* watch. That *Tejano* go straight to the ranch of Farias. Then he cross the border an' ride toward Cayuse. He dodge the patrol riders like he ees not want to be seen."

"Then it's some skunk tryin' to bluff me," said Ike Babcock, his eyes narrowing a little. "Well, I'll make double sure. Then I'll fetch you enough guns to supply all Mexico. Here's how!"

"*Salude, señor!*"

BLOODSTAINED TARP

A STRANGER RODE INTO the little cow town of Cayuse. He was a tall, well-made man in his early thirties. He had gray eyes and tow-colored hair, and he looked as if he needed money. But his saddle was a full-stamped, double-rigged job, made for hard wear rather than for show. His spurs and bit were silver-mounted. And the horse he rode was a big black gelding that any man would be proud to ride. The horse had a blotched brand on the left shoulder.

He stabled his horse and left his chaps with his saddle. Then he walked back up the street toward the restaurant, which was a squalid little place run by a Mexican couple. He started to pass Luther Johns's Trading Post, but seemed to change his mind. He looked at the assortment of odds and ends in the window. Six-guns, bridles, a secondhand saddle, a carbine. Hunks of ore. A miner's pick and gold pan.

He looked at the fly-specked sign propped against the saddle.

"Luther Johns will buy, sell, or trade anything," read the cowboy. He walked inside the store.

Luther Johns, his right hand hidden under the counter, looked at the stranger with his one bloodshot eye.

"What'll it be, stranger?"

The bronzed cowboy grinned faintly and took a big silver watch from his pocket.

"Figgered you might lend me somethin' on it. I don't want to sell it. Just hock it. I hope to land a job around here."

"Broke?" asked Luther Johns, studying the stranger's face. The man who had held him up two weeks ago had eyes the same color. He talked with the same, slow drawl. Yet there were other gray-eyed Texans. A deal was a deal. Still there—

"If I had money would I be hockin' a watch that belonged to my dead father?"

"I'll let you have five on that six-shooter."

"A man's gun is about the last thing he parts with when he's a plumb stranger in a strange land. Let me have ten dollars on this watch, and I'll be obliged."

Luther Johns nodded. After all, the man could not win anything by robbing him now. He had his money hidden under the floor. There was less than a hundred dollars in the safe. Besides, if this was the hold-up man, then he would set a little trap for the fellow. Luther Johns's right hand came up from under the counter, empty. He examined the watch. Then he handed over ten dollars.

"Looking for work?"

"I shore am, mister." His tone sounded sincere.

"Jack Jackson of the Cross X is in town. He might put you on, if he likes your looks. He'll be sitting in a poker game up the street, most likely."

"I'm obliged. I'll git the wrinkles outta my stomach, first. Jackson? Is that the feller they call Jack of Spades?"

"That's him."

"He ramrods King Kennedy's spread?"

"You seem well informed, stranger."

"A man don't have to read the newspapers to know Kennedy's Cross X outfit." He grinned and pocketed his money.

When the cowboy had gone into the restaurant, Luther Johns locked his store and went up the street to the saloon. He called Jackson away from a stud-poker game.

"Stranger in town, Jack, looking for work. He fits the description of the man that stuck me up."

"A man with a twenty-five-thousand-dollar roll ain't huntin' work, Luther."

"Not unless he's smart."

"I git you. I'll put him on. What's his name?"

"I didn't ask him. Didn't want to scare him off. Hire him. Keep an eye on him."

"Don't worry. If he's the son that spilled my herd, he'll be wearin' holes in his hide before long. Any news from Ike?"

"Not yet. There's rumors, but no news."

"What kind o' rumors?" asked Jackson.

"The two border patrol men that stopped here and left a letter for him hinted that Ike had brought up his last drive out of Mexico. They're after his hide."

"That's no news. They've been after that for years. Ike ain't easy to ketch."

"But these two men are newcomers. There's a dozen new men on the border, and they have orders to plug the holes. They mean business. The gray-haired officer said to tell Ike, if I saw him, that it took more than a hundred-dollar bill to buy him and his partner."

"Ike never tried to buy any man for a measly hundred. He's never tried to buy off the law."

"I suppose you still believe there's a Santa Claus, too, don't you, Jack?" said the one-eyed man.

"I know Ike Babcock," replied Jackson, "and I know that he don't buy his way across the border. I don't like Ike any more than you do, but he's too game a sport to use money to git cattle across the line. If that border patrol man says Ike tried to bribe him, he lies. Is that yore man, comin' in the door?"

"That's the man."

The gray-eyed stranger walked up to them. Luther Johns nodded to him.

"I was just telling Jackson you were looking for a job. Jack, this is— What's the name, stranger?"

"Tom Stroud. You need men, mister?" he asked Jackson.

"That depends, Stroud. It takes a shore-enough cowhand to work for me. The Cross X pays fightin' wages. Savvy what I mean?"

Tom Stroud nodded, grinning faintly. When a man drew fighting wages with a cow outfit, he hired out to do more than plain cow-punching. He hired out to take his chances.

"I've drawed fightin' pay before, Jackson."

"Where?"

"I ain't sayin', mister."

Jackson nodded. "Yore back tracks is yore own, Stroud. The outfit is camped about ten miles from here, on the main trail to the ranch. You can't miss it. I'll give you a note to the wagon boss. Be there some time tomorrow. We pay a hundred a month and furnish cartridges. Got a bed?"

"Lost my bed on my way here," replied the cowboy.

"Luther will fix you up with one. There's three—four beds at his tradin' post. If you need money, Luther will give you fifty dollars. Have a drink?"

"Too soon after eatin', thanks. I'll take about ten dollars in advance. Enough to git my watch outta hock. And I'll mosey on down an' git that bed which I'll pay for when I earn it. I'm obliged for the drink, but, to tell the truth, I ain't much of a hand at it. I'll buy one for you gents, though."

Luther Johns and Jackson took a drink. Tom Stroud took a cigar wrapped in tinfoil which he put in the pocket of his flannel shirt. Then he and Luther Johns went down the street to the store.

As Luther Johns was unlocking the door, a man on a big, sweat-marked roan rode past. He called out a hearty "Howdy, Luther!" and rode on to the barn.

"Who's that?" asked Tom Stroud.

"That," said Luther Johns, whose one eye had been watching the stranger named Tom Stroud, "is none other than Ike Babcock. Perhaps you've heard of him?"

"Gosh, yes. So that's Ike Babcock! Gosh, he's a big gent. Bigger'n a skinned mule."

"And as dangerous as a grizzly," added Luther Johns as he opened the door and propped it open with a rusty shotgun barrel.

"I always wanted to meet Ike Babcock."

Luther gave him his watch and forty dollars. "If you're staying in town tonight, you'll need some change."

A rear storeroom behind the store held a litter of saddles, bridles, saddle blankets, chaps, guns, and beds as well.

"This is the morgue, Stroud," explained the one-eyed man. "Some of the stuff was pawned, as you pawned your watch, and never redeemed. But the bulk of it belongs to men who died with their boots on, here in Cayuse. Residents, now, of our local boot hill. Take your pick of the bed rolls. They're all good beds. Half price on any that are bloodstained." And he chuckled in a grisly fashion.

Tom Stroud examined the rolled, tarp-covered beds. One of the tarps was stained with blood. On it had been marked, with black paint, a brand. The brand was Lazy S.

"I'll take this un," said Tom Stroud, as he examined

the blankets and then rolled and tied the bed again in its bloodstained tarp. "Half off for bloodstains makes it how much?"

The light in the storeroom was none too good, so Luther Johns did not notice that the cowboy's hands were a little unsteady as he examined the bed. And the one-eyed storekeeper was too drunk to detect the husky note in Tom Stroud's voice.

"Ten dollars is the price."

"Here's the money. I'll take the bed. Who owned it?"

"A young cowboy that got killed here a few weeks ago. One of the Cross X cowboys. They're a tough lot. Those cowboys know how to turn this town wrong side out when they—"

"Yuh in there, Luther?" bellowed a loud voice from the front of the store.

"Be right with you, Ike!"

Luther Johns, followed by the cowboy carrying his newly acquired bed roll, quit the storeroom and went into the store.

"Thought another burglar had yuh hogtied somewheres," said the big cowman. "I want some Durham an' brown papers. Likewise all the licorice-flavored chawin' gum in the store. And a box o' .45 shells. On top o' that, git out some bandages an' idodine, because the boy that's comin' in after a while has a hole in his arm. Git the bandage stuff up to the saloon. Why, howdy, stranger," he added, as Tom Stroud, the bed across his shoulder, came in from the storeroom.

Tom Stroud nodded and grinned. Then he went on out and down the street to the barn.

"Who's the stranger, Luther?"

"Some cowboy named Tom Stroud. Just hired out to

the Cross X. You ever see him before, Ike?"

"Not to remember, and mostly I don't forgit a face or a brand. That his black horse in the barn? I reckon. Rides a Miles City rig, but it's a rim-fire, not a Montana rig. Tom Stroud? I knowed a Tom Stroud once. He's a likely lookin' cowboy. Now lemme have them ca'tridges an' that tobacco and the gum. The kind Kid Brady chaws."

"Since when have you turned gum-chewer, Ike?"

"Ain't turned. I'm jobbin' the Kid. Him an' King Kennedy is due here some time tonight. The Kid an' him has been on a secret *pasear* some place. The Kid will be outta gum. I'm buyin' up all the red sody pop. And I'm goin' to have some fun with that gun-totin' young scalawag. Just watch him fight his head when he finds out that Cayuse ain't got ary licorish gum ner red pop." He laughed heartily as he broke open the box of cartridges and filled the many empty loops of his wide cartridge belt.

"You had some trouble, Ike?"

"Plenty. That is, some. A little, you might say. Lost three good men, and another un got his gun arm busted. Two days ago. A bunch of Yaquis an' mongrels from the hills tried to steal my herd. There must 'a' been fifty of 'em."

"Then you lost the drive?"

"Lost nothin' but our sleep. Them cattle will be here before daylight if they don't sulk on the boys. Is Kennedy in yet?"

"No. I didn't know he was expected."

"I sent him word four days ago. And I want the money here tonight. We got to git back. I'm countin' them cattle over to Jackson at sunrise in the mornin'. Is Jackson's outfit here to take delivery?"

"They're camped ten miles from here. Jackson don't expect those cattle for five or six days."

"Well, he's gettin' 'em in the mornin'. Jackson don't expect 'em? You didn't expect 'em? Still I got word to Kennedy in plenty time. I sent a man with a letter to him. He delivered it at the Cross X Ranch. Now, why—"

"You positive the letter was delivered, Ike?"

"I sent out a man I kin trust. He wanted to go to Phoenix to have a tooth pulled, so I told him not to report back. But— You suppose he got stopped, Luther? That the letter never got to Kennedy? Reckon I'm bein' pulled into a trap?" The grin left his homely face.

"Stranger things have happened even to men as smart as Ike Babcock," replied Luther Johns thinly, and he rolled one of his *marijuana* cigarettes.

THE LAW

IT WAS ABOUT MIDNIGHT. Tom Stroud, Jackson, and the rest of the Cross X cowboys were in Cayuse. Their saddled horses, cinches loosened, were in the big feed yard behind the barn.

Luther Johns smoked one cigarette after another as he stood at the bar. Jackson was in a black mood. Even the big Ike Babcock's grin seemed a little strained.

"Somethin's gone wrong, Luther," said Ike Babcock. "I kinda feel it in my bones.

"At daylight, Luther, I want the cash money laid on the line. I had to put the bulk o' these dogies in Kennedy's iron in order to git 'em acrost. I told them border patrol men they was Kennedy's strays an' I was gatherin' 'em."

Jackson eyed Ike Babcock.

"You work almighty slick, Ike. One o' my boys seen that bunch o' cattle you been holdin' this side o' the border. They're stuff from that herd that got stampeded."

"Kin you prove that, Jackson?"

"No," admitted Jackson; "I got no proof."

"A man hadn't oughta make statements he can't back with actual proof, Jackson. There's a bunch o' cattle due here in the mornin', and yo're takin' delivery. Kennedy contracted for 'em. Yeah, Kennedy. What's the use in sparrin' around? Luther's just a fence. And if King Kennedy or any other man thinks he kin put over anything on Ike Babcock, they better read up some on how to do it. I want the money for them cattle in the mornin'. Cash money. No tricks."

"That part of it is up to King," said Jackson. "I'm here to take delivery. Got my men here. Looks like Luther was due to pay off."

"I'll not pay," snarled Luther Johns. "Thirty thousand dollars out of my bank roll? Just guess again, Jackson. I lost the last time."

"You wasn't the only loser," Jackson reminded him sourly. "I'm loser, just as much as you are."

The three of them stood apart from the crowd. In the heat of their discussion they paid no heed to Tom Stroud, who sat at an empty card table near by, apparently asleep. Tom Stroud's battered hat was down across his eyes. A cold cigarette hung from his lips. There was an empty beer glass on the table. Nobody paid him any attention.

If he saw King Kennedy and Kid Brady come in through the swing-doors, he gave no sign.

Kennedy's heavy face wore a week's growth of whiskers. His eyes were bloodshot, sunken in purple sockets. His lips twitched convulsively. He grabbed a bottle of whisky and gulped it down, the two hands that held the bottle shaking, thick wrists marked by raw scars.

Kid Brady tried to grin, but failed. He showed only a set of buckteeth between bruised, swollen lips. One eye was discolored, swollen shut. And his gun hand was bandaged crudely.

"You look," said Ike Babcock, "for all the world like a pair o' tom-cats come home."

"Come on." King Kennedy's voice was like the surly growl of a bear. He led the way back to the private room.

Luther Johns, Ike Babcock, Jackson, and Kid Brady followed.

King Kennedy motioned for Kid Brady to lock the door, as they sat down.

"Git my note?" asked Ike Babcock.

King Kennedy eyed him coldly. Kid Brady stood with his back against the locked door.

"I got the note, Babcock," growled Kennedy. "Fetch the money?"

"No."

"Goin' back on yore contract, Kennedy?"

"No. I'm takin' delivery on the cattle."

"Them cattle is delivered C.O.D., Kennedy."

Ike Babcock's eyes hardened.

"I'm takin' delivery, Babcock," repeated King Kennedy.

"But you ain't payin'?"

"That's it, Babcock. Twice is two times too many."

"Meanin' just how?"

"Meanin' that I start out from the ranch with the cash. We get stuck up. Ambushed. Cleaned of every dollar I was bringin' here. Thirty thousand dollars. And if you know any prayers, Babcock, say 'em. Say 'em fast."

Ike Babcock sat back in his chair. He lifted his hat and scratched his uncombed hair. His grin widened.

"Tuck in yore shirt, Kennedy. Don't go makin' them fancy plays. You an' Kid Brady shore look like you'd been through a few tough nights, but if you figger I'm the cause, yo're loco. What happened?"

"You know what happened, Babcock!"

"I sent you word that I'd have yore cattle here in the mornin'. I was a little early in makin' delivery. I sent the note by one of yore own men that you sent down with me. A slim gent called Bean-pole."

"Then either you lie or Bean-pole has changed into a short, heavy-set gent with one game leg."

"A short, game-legged man? Gray hair? Blue-eyed? Has a wart on his left cheek?" Ike Babcock leaned across the table.

"That's him."

"Then Bean-pole is in jail. The feller that delivered that note is a border patrol man. His name's Cassidy, and he's smart. What happened from then on?"

"I started out from the ranch with the money. I took along Kid Brady. Some men bushwhacked us. Stuck us up. It was dark. They put us in a cabin an' kept us there. This evenin' at dark they turned us loose. Not once did we git a look at the men that had us penned up. They fed us after dark. The cabin where we stayed hadn't any windows. The grub was shoved in through a hole made in the door. They kept me handcuffed. The Kid was better off. He'd got his hand busted by a gun barrel, and they didn't put handcuffs on him. There's the story, if you ain't heard it before, Babcock. You got to prove to me that you didn't frame the deal. You got to prove that or you'll never leave this room alive."

There came a pounding on the door. Every man in the room stiffened in his chair. Every man looked at each other, suspicion in their eyes. Ike Babcock rolled a smoke, grinning. He looked at King Kennedy, who had drawn his gun.

"Don't go off half-cock, King. Ask who's out there." He leaned back in his chair, and his spurred boot heels rested on the table. Of them all, he was the only one who seemed at ease.

"You trickin' me again, Babcock?" snarled Kennedy. "Because, if you are, I'll—"

"Open that door!" commanded a voice out in the hallway that led to the card rooms. "Open up, there, or I'll break down the door. It's the United States government talking! Open up, in the name of the law! Open up, or I'll break down the door!"

"Might be a good idea," said Ike Babcock, "to let in some law. If I was you, Kid, I'd open that door."

Kid Brady looked at Kennedy.

"Let 'em in," growled Kennedy.

"Come in, gents." Kid Brady unlocked the door.

Two men wearing badges came into the room, guns drawn. Big Ike Babcock chuckled as he got to his feet. He grinned at the law officers.

"Have chairs, gents. Now, doggone, there ain't no extra chairs. Reckon you'll have to stand up, boys."

King Kennedy's florid face paled a little as he looked at the older of the two border patrol men. Then he shot a sidelong glance at Ike Babcock, who raked a spur lazily across the table top. Ike's grin was wide, genial.

"You men are under arrest," snapped the older of the two border patrol officers.

"What charges?" drawled Ike.

"You know the charges, Babcock. Handling wet cattle. I captured your messenger and delivered in person the order that you were bringing to Kennedy two thousand head of cattle and that you wanted the money tonight before midnight. Jackson has his men out there in the saloon, ready to take delivery of the cattle. Babcock, your drive of stolen cattle is due here at daylight. What have you rustlers got to say about that? Any alibis?"

"I done gathered some o' Kennedy's cattle," said Ike Babcock unhurriedly. "Kennedy will nacherally pay me for the trouble. But they ain't stolen cattle. I got a bill o' sale for all the cattle I ever sold. And that herd is in King Kennedy's iron."

"Freshly branded, Babcock. You sold those cattle to King Kennedy. Can you deny that?"

"I ain't been paid for 'em, Cassidy. An', from the way Kennedy talks, that ain't the half of it. You admit you kinda intercepted that note I sent. That right?"

"You heard me say so."

"Well, mister, somebody kidnapped Kennedy and Kid Brady and robbed 'em o' some money. You was the only man that was on to the fact that Kennedy was ridin' here, a few days ago, with money on him. I'm askin' you, mister, and I want the right answer—did you two gents rob King Kennedy?"

"You're talking like a drunken man," snapped the patrol man, Cassidy. "Up with your hands all of you. Face that wall. And if I find what I hope to find, you'll all do time. Frisk 'em, Chick. Either Kennedy or Ike Babcock will have thirty thousand dollars in marked money. Or you might find it on Luther Johns. Frisk 'em."

Ike Babcock lifted his arms. He grinned at Kid Brady.

The Kid grinned back, after a fashion.

"Marked money?" snarled Luther Johns. "Say, are you two fools drunk, or is this a joke?"

"We aren't drunk, Johns," growled the man named Cassidy, "and don't play jokes. Keep those hands up in the air."

They were searched, one by one. King Kennedy, purple with rage, cursed them heartily.

"Don't git yore blood hot, King," advised Ike. "Fellers like you die off from high blood pressure."

Kid Brady chewed his gum. He wondered what it was all about. Fast with a gun, but slow-witted, Kid Brady.

Jackson muttered under his breath. Now and then his glittering eyes looked at Ike Babcock. Ike would grin.

Luther Johns was thinking as hard as his clever brain could work. He cursed the two officers as they searched his pockets.

Finally the ordeal was over. Cassidy glared at Ike Babcock. Ike grinned back at him.

"It looks," said Ike Babcock, "like a horse on you boys. Now, I just wonder if you got enough sportin' blood in you to buy the drinks?"

At that moment a man showed up in the doorway. He was a roughly dressed cowboy.

"Ike," he said in an excited tone, "bad news. The herd's stampeded!"

A DANGEROUS GAME

JACKSON'S THIN SMILE WAS meant for Ike Babcock. It was one of those lipless smiles that is like a slap in the face for the man for whom it's intended. But Ike Babcock laughed and hit the table with a hard, calloused palm.

"It's a horse on me, boys. My herd is done spilled. Cassidy, it looks like there ain't much for you to go on, either. You found no thirty thousand dollars on any of us. Them men you hired to take over that herd has spilled 'em dogies all over the landscape."

Cassidy turned to his younger partner.

"Handcuff 'em, Chick. They can't get away with this." His eyes were hard, narrowed. "They've hidden the money somewheres. Babcock has turned loose his cattle. But we still have that note written to Kennedy from Babcock."

"You have the note?" growled Kennedy.

Cassidy smiled faintly. "I have the original. You got just a copy that Chick made."

Ike Babcock's laugh filled the room. Luther Johns rolled one of his *marijuana* cigarettes, and his one eye watched Ike Babcock.

Now Luther Johns looked at Cassidy, as the irate border patrol man got out his handcuffs.

"I wouldn't make any mistakes, if I were you, Cassidy. Be sure what you're doing."

"I know what I'm doing, you outlawed shyster."

"Then go ahead. But that note won't be worth a plugged Mexican dobe dollar in court."

"No? We'll see about that. Handcuff 'em all, Chick. We'll call their bluff."

"It so happens," said Luther Johns, "that we're not bluffing. I'm an attorney. Rather, I was an attorney until I was disbarred from practice. Nevertheless, I know the law, backward and forward, inside and out, and I can prove in court that you found no money, no marked money, on any of us. I thank you for the information that Kennedy's money that he gets from the bank is marked. That covers that point.

"Concerning the cattle. You have no cattle as evidence. And even if you did grab off those cattle, they're all in the Cross X iron, which leaves you nothing in the way of evidence."

"I have a letter from Ike Babcock, written to King Kennedy, that tells Kennedy he's delivering him two thousand head of cattle. Mexican cattle. That'll tie you all up."

"Guess once more," replied Luther Johns. "That letter will be thrown out of court."

"Yeah? Why?"

"Because it will be absolutely proved in any court that Ike Babcock cannot write. He signs his checks with a mark and a thumb-print. Put away those bracelets and behave. You're licked, Mr. Law. Licked. Out-foxed. Go learn something, then come back along the border below Cayuse. Make a pinch now, and it will cost you and the Chick gent your little measly jobs. Get out. Stay away from Cayuse or you'll run into a lot of bad luck."

It was a long speech for the taciturn Luther Johns, one-time criminal lawyer, later a convict, later an ex-convict. And Cassidy, who knew that Luther Johns never bluffed unless he had the cards, put away his handcuffs.

"We might as well go, Chick," he said grimly. "But, before we go, you all listen to me. I'll get you all before I'm finished. I was sent down here to plug the holes in the border. I never yet quit a job till it was finished."

"I'll ride down the road a ways with you, Cassidy," said Ike Babcock. "I hate to see you go off in a huff, that a way. And after makin' the kind of a play you made, it might not be plumb safe to ride alone in the moonlight. I'll ride a ways with you."

Ike Babcock ignored Kennedy's black scowl. He answered Jackson's thin smile with a throaty chuckle. Ike was on his feet, hitching up his warped overalls.

Cassidy looked at the men there in the smoke-filled room. He met the puckered gaze of Ike Babcock.

"Thanks, Babcock; I'd like your company."

Big Ike Babcock looked at the cowboy who had brought news of the stampede. The cowboy nodded briefly and went away. Now Ike Babcock faced Kennedy and Luther Johns.

"I'll meet you back here in time for breakfast. Be here, Kennedy. Jackson, if ary one o' yore men foller us, he'll meet up with bad luck. See you later."

"Babcock," said Cassidy, as he and the big cattleman and "Chick" got on their horses, "is this a trap?"

"If you think it is, Cassidy, I'll stay behind."

"I'll chance it."

They were on the edge of town when they caught up with a lone rider. Ike Babcock immediately hailed him.

"Who are you, mister?"

"I'm Tom Stroud. You met me this evenin'.

"Shore enough. Son o' the Tom Stroud I knewed in Texas. Better turn back."

"I'd a heap rather ride a ways. I need some air. Taken on too many back at the saloon. Me and my pony need exercise."

"You workin' for Kennedy?"

"I hired out to him. Does that bar me from ridin' along with you gents?"

"I told you I knowed yore dad. Tom Stroud's boy is always plumb welcome to ride with me."

They rode throughout the night. Ike Babcock led the way, swinging off the main trail.

"What's the idea, Babcock?" asked Cassidy.

"Might be some lead poison if we kep' to the big trail. I know what I'm talkin' about. Foller me an' ride hard."

They rode hard. An hour and a half and they were at the camp of the border patrol riders. Ike Babcock had led them to their own camp by a twisting short cut that led through a deep canyon and rimmed out near the canyon head.

"Cassidy," said Ike Babcock, "King Kennedy is bad medicine. Watch him. If we'd kep' to the main trail tonight, there'd 'a been shootin' and plenty of it. You have a talk tomorrow with the chief of yore outfit, an' he'll tell you some things you need to know about this part of the border country. So long."

"Just a minute, Babcock," spoke Cassidy. "I know I've made a bad mistake. I know you only by reputation. I'm believing what you've told me. And I'm thanking you for your escort. Stop at my camp any time. And the meals are free, if you wash the dishes."

He held out his hand. Ike Babcock gripped it.

"We'll git along, Cassidy. You an' the Chick boy be plenty watchful when you ride, that's all. Kennedy's as poison as a rattler. Jackson is bad medicine. Luther Johns would kill a man for what's in his pockets. Just remember I told you. So long."

Ike Babcock and Tom Stroud rode back toward town. Ike broke the silence.

"What made you come along, Tom Stroud?"

"I come for the fresh air, Ike."

"I knowed yore dad plenty. Him and me was kinda pardners once. Then we split up. Got in a fool argument o' some kind. Quit speakin'. Quit speakin' to one another for five years. Then I found him dead one mornin', near my ranch. They tried me for his murder.

Is it because you think I killed him that you wanted to be ridin' along with me tonight? You an' me alone?"

"Supposin' it was?" asked Tom Stroud.

"I didn't kill yore dad. I'd hate to be crowded into hurtin' the son of a man that was once my pardner. As a matter o' fact, young feller, I'll give you a free shot at me if you think I killed a man that had been like my own brother to me. If you think I killed yore father, have at it. A free shot."

From another man it would have sounded melodramatic. But Ike Babcock had not changed the tone of his voice. He kept riding along, talking in a pleasant drawl. Big, raw-boned, rough-hewn, tough as old jerky wrapped around barb wire.

"I never figgered you killed my father. That's why I'm with you tonight. I was scared you'd take a trail where some o' them snakes was hidin'. Kennedy wants them two law officers and he wants you. I heard Jackson give orders. Takin' that short cut left his bushwhackers holdin' the empty sack. I aimed to help you, that's all. Them gents got fooled."

Ike Babcock laughed. "Like snipe hunters."

Tom Stroud agreed with a nod. "Like snipe hunters. Only they don't pack lanterns."

"For a man that ain't been in the country long, you know aplenty about things."

"I got eyes, ears, and a nose."

"Well, you'll need 'em. Jackson will be watchin' you every minute. Luther Johns is watchin' you. I'm watching' you, so far as that goes. I don't savvy yore game, Tom Stroud, but it's about as safe as monkeyin' with blastin' powder an' a lighted fuse. We'll turn off the trail right here."

"What for?" asked Tom Stroud.

"You kin do better workin' for me than you kin do workin' with Jackson."

"How do you mean?"

Ike Babcock lighted his cigarette. The glow of the cupped match showed his grin, his puckered eyes, his rugged, homely features. Then he let the match go out.

"A feller with gray eyes. A Texican," he said, as if musing out loud. "A gent about yore build. Luther Johns never forgits a detail. It's part o' his game to remember a man's voice, his eyes, the way he handles hisse'f. Even if the feller's face is hid by a black silk handkerchief. Savvy what I mean?"

"I reckon," said Tom Stroud, "that I savvy. But I—"

"I just hired you away from the Cross X outfit because I don't want of Tom Stroud's boy gittin' shot in the back. Yo're workin' for me from here on. An' tonight we got cattle to move."

"Meanin' how?"

"Meanin' that my drive wasn't stampeded, not a-tall. We had two herds comin' up the trail. Cassidy's men—or was it yore men—picked the wrong herd. A bunch o' culls I'd cut out. The main herd gits delivered at daylight to Luther Johns at Cayuse. Directly we git the herd movin' along good, me an' you goes back to Cayuse to collect thirty thousand dollars in cash money. And I'm warnin' you, Tom, robbin' Luther Johns or Kennedy, and robbin' of Ike Babcock is a heap different. Have I hired a new ramrod?"

"It looks like you kinda shanghaied me." Tom Stroud grinned.

At sunrise a herd of cattle was counted over to Jackson. Riding up on the point of the trail herd that drifted out of the dawn on to the Cayuse range was Tom Stroud. Jackson glared at him. Tom Stroud counted off fifty dollars.

"That's what you advanced me, Jackson. I changed my mind an' hired out to Ike Babcock. He pays better wages."

"You'll earn 'em, Stroud. Got any close kinfolks? Mebbyso a wife or a sweetheart?"

"Supposin' I have, Jackson?"

"Leave their name an' address with Luther Johns. He buries folks that git planted at Cayuse."

"So I done heard. Think I'll stake out a three-by-six claim there, Jackson?"

"I've done paid yore funeral expenses, Stroud."

"Which is shore accommodatin'. When does the funeral come off?" Tom Stroud's hand was on his gun.

"Most any ol' time, Stroud."

"Supposin' we git back to cattle countin', Jackson. Or would you like to git a bullet in yore middle?"

"Yore funeral is paid for, Stroud. We'll plant you when we git around to it. Today is Friday. Bad luck to kill a man on a Friday."

Tom Stroud grinned. "Count them cattle. I might kill you or Kennedy or Luther Johns or Kid Brady on any day in the week. Tell that to yore *compadres.* I'm not scared to deal 'em out face up. Want yore medicine now, Jackson? I'll give you a break for yore gun. Better take it. If you don't, I'm seein' you hung some day."

"You seein' me hung? When you put on more age, you'll learn yore A B C's at this game. You and yore pardner, Ike Babcock. When I git around to it, Stroud, I'll kill you. Not this mornin'."

"So we'll just count cattle, Jackson."

"We'll just count cattle, Stroud."

They counted the cattle that were stringing past. Jackson tallied every hundred head by tying a knot in his bridle reins. Tom Stroud was tallying with matches, changing a match from the right hand pocket of his jumper to the left-hand pocket.

"Tally eight," growled Jackson.

"Tally eight," said Tom Stroud.

Cow punchers, cowmen. Counting cattle by tens as they were strung out from the broken country, between the granite boulders of a canyon. The cattle were spreading out, leg-weary, footsore, gaunt-flanked, red-eyed, headed for grass and water.

Dust curled up in sluggish puffs from under the hoofs of the trail herd. Now and then a steer bawled. Horses were sweat-marked, shuffling with lowered heads. Men were unshaven, covered with powdered dust, tight-lipped, their eyes like holes in a burned blanket. Those men had not slept for forty-eight hours. They rubbed tobacco in their eyes to keep awake. One or two dozed in the saddle. Those were Ike Babcock's riders from Mexico. Men who could live on dry jerky and alkali water and sleep with a saddle for a pillow. The hardest, toughest cowboys that could be hand-picked in the Southwest.

Tom Stroud looked them over. Texas cowboys, men from Montana, Wyoming, Colorado. Mexicans. Native Californians. Renegades, all. But the cream of the cow country. All wore the service-worn chaps, overalls, and jumper. Their hats, for the most part, were old and out of shape. Their boots were dusty, worn. Their *tapaderas* were scarred and broken by cat's-claw and mesquite. Most of them used a breast strap and breeching on their saddles to keep their rigs from slipping when roping and riding in the rough country. A few of them wore gloves. The hands of the others were scabbed by the thorns and cacti. Every horse was scarred around the legs.

Men and horses looked exactly what they were. Wild cowboys. Fast horses accustomed to rocks, brush, and cacti. Hard-bitten, uncomplaining. Every man wore a six-gun. On every saddle was a Winchester.

These riders all needed soap and water and clean clothes. Tom Stroud looked them over with a nod of approval.

The Cross X men were of almost the same breed. Better fed, better taken care of, perhaps. But not better mounted. Every man working for Ike Babcock rode a top horse. Every man had a good rig. The Mexicans favored silver-mounted headstalls, bits, and spurs. Flat-horned saddles with low cantles. Here and there a Miles City saddle. Round shirts, full-stamped or plain. Center-fire and three-quarter rigs. The center-fire saddle also earmarked the Californian with his fifty-foot rawhide reata and his spade bit.

No sign of Ike Babcock, there in the dust-powdered sunrise. Ike was in town.

"Tally what, Jackson?" asked Tom Stroud as the last of the cattle passed them by.

"Two thousand and twelve head."

"I made it two thousand and five. They're yourn, Jackson. Take 'em away!"

Jackson nodded and rode away without a word. Tom Stroud rode his horse up on a knoll. The Babcock cowboys were drifting back, one by one, or in little groups. They looked at Tom Stroud. A red-headed cowboy handed Tom Stroud a tally book and a six-gun.

"They go with the job, I reckon. The feller that packed 'em a few days ago got shot. I been kinda straw boss. Ike told me we was takin' orders from you. Said yore name was Tom Stroud, and that from now on we was yore hired hands."

"I hired out as ramrod," Tom told them, taking the gun and the blood-spattered tally book. "And we better git somethings kinda straightened out right now. You boys don't know me. Some of you been with Ike Babcock a long time, I reckon. You wonder why he's hired me. I'm sorry, boys, but, not knowin' why, I can't say. I'll do my best to give you all a square deal. I don't know the country so good, but I hope we won't have to change horses every mornin' before we git in off circle. You boys treat me white; I'll do the same by you. And if there is ary man in this spread that has got a horn drooped right now, let him beller. Is there ary man don't want to work under me?"

No man spoke. Tom Stroud shoved the tally book in his pocket and looked at the ivory-handled gun that had been given him. The gun was empty. He loaded it slowly, a queer smile on his face. Then he cocked the gun.

"You, mister, with the black hat, head for town. Find Ike Babcock and tell him I fired you. That goes for the gent with the checkered shirt and that Mexican with the red-colored sash. I know all of you. Yo're all fired. Git yore time from Ike Babcock. Then tell Jackson that you come home to roost. Clear out, or I'll smoke you out!"

LOCOED COWBOY

TOM STROUD HAD TAKEN over a hard job. He knew that when he rode to the trail camp on the river bank with the men who were paid to take his orders. His crew was as tough a bunch of men as could be gathered. They were watching him, waiting to see how he would handle them. Waiting to find out if he was going to make a mistake.

The rope corral held a remuda of good horses. There was a cook in overalls, a six-gun hung on him, working over the Dutch ovens. A grizzled, stoop-shouldered, stout man, the cook. His flour-sack apron needed washing. He needed a haircut and shave and a clean shirt. His shapeless hat was tilted sideways across a pair of keen brownish eyes. He had the legs and manners of a cowhand. His hair was white. He puffed a corncob pipe. But when he lifted the lid of a Dutch oven with his pothook, there was revealed meat and bread and beans that were good enough for any man's appetite. And the simmering coffee in the huge blackened coffee-pot was the kind that only a cowboy knows how to make.

"Come an' git 'em, wart hawgs, or I'll th'ow 'er away!"

"Ketch yore town horses after we eat, boys," said Tom Stroud. "I don't know how you boys feel, but I kin eat grub."

It was nearing noon when they rode into town. Jackson and his men had left Cayuse to take over the cattle. The town looked empty, deserted. They stopped at the saloon, and Tom laid a twenty-dollar bill on the bar.

"Give the boys what they want. Where's Ike Babcock?"

"In the back room with Kennedy and Kid Brady and Luther Johns."

Tom started to leave the bar.

"Hold on, Stroud," said the saloon man. "I got orders to keep everybody away from the back room."

"Whose orders, mister?"

"King Kennedy's orders."

Tom Stroud grinned widely. "I don't take Kennedy's

orders. I'm workin' for Ike Babcock."

"That makes no difference. I own this place. What I say goes. King ain't to be disturbed by no drunken cowboys."

Tom turned to his men. "You boys will need some money. I'm gittin' it from Ike. Ride herd on this liquor-dealin' jasper, will you? Kinda keep 'im busy."

"Have at 'er, Tom," said a bearded man. "We're takin' yore orders. Don't mind this fat-faced bar thing."

"I'll see you all directly, boys."

Tom Stroud, his spurs jingling, walked back to the card room. Without knocking, he opened the door with his left hand. In his right hand was the ivory-handled gun.

He paused in the doorway, ready for anything. He saw the black scowl on Kennedy's face. He saw Luther Johns's one eye glitter menacingly. Kid Brady chewed his wad of gum. Ike Babcock waved a welcome with a hairy paw.

"Come in, Tom," said Ike Babcock. "Shut the door behind you. I just was tellin' 'em I'd hired you away from Jackson. Take a chair an' set down. Put up yore gun."

"The boys is in town, Ike. They need money. Luther Johns might do some rushin' business if he'd open up his store. They all want underwear an' shirts and so on. Kin you pay 'em, Ike?"

Ike Babcock handed over a roll of money. "Here's the pay roll, Tom. Here's the book that tells how much they each got comin'. Pay 'em what they ask for, inside what they got comin'. Put the change in yore pocket. Drink?"

"I'll whittle on a bottle o' Kid Brady's red pop."

"Not today, cowboy," said Kid Brady. "I don't split pop or gum or anything with any man. I got a notion to—"

"Dry up," growled Kennedy. "I'll get the notions, then pass 'em on. Keep yore trap shut and yore gun where it belongs. Luther, go down and open up the store. Cowboys in town. Ike, are we talking business or not? Send this Stroud cowboy out with the pay roll, and we'll talk turkey. I want this thing settled."

"In which case," said Tom Stroud, "I'll set down. Brady, if you feel lucky, pull that gun, and we'll have it out here and now. I'm not leavin' Ike Babcock here alone with you gents. I hired out to him. I'm doin' this on my own hook, even if Ike fires me for it. I'm keepin' my gun in my hand. And it'll kill the first man that makes the wrong play. That goes for Luther Johns, Kid Brady, and Kennedy. No man kin murder Ike Babcock and git away with it."

"What do you mean, Tom?" asked Ike Babcock.

"I mean I had a show-down with Jackson this mornin'. I fired three Jackson men that was workin' for you. I'm layin' my cards on the table. I know Jackson's game. I know Luther Johns's game. I know King Kennedy's game. And I'm workin' as ramrod for Ike Babcock. You hired me, Ike. You ain't firin' me. I'm roddin' my spread as I want. And, before I'm done, I'll take any of you on. I'm one man against aplenty, but I'll git my bite while the others git a meal."

"So that locoed cowboy is yore new ramrod, Ike?" King Kennedy sneered.

"You heard what he said, Kennedy." Ike Babcock was looking at Tom Stroud, his big mouth grinning queerly, a quizzical look in his puckered eyes.

"He's loco!" growled Kennedy, his jowled face purpling.

"You heard what he said, Kennedy. I done hired him.

Looks he's stayin' hired."

"He's the man that stuck me up," snarled Luther Johns.

"That'd be hard to prove," replied Tom Stroud. "I been told that you do the plantin' at the Cayuse boot hill. I been told that my funeral expenses was already paid for. Bein' a man that takes his own part and asks no favors, I'm payin' now for four plantin's. A hundred bucks a throw. Put down the names. Kennedy. Yeah, King Kennedy. Jackson. Kid Brady. And last, but not least, Luther Johns. Here's four hundred dollars, you one-eyed buzzard. Keep it an' mark it on yore dirty ledger. Kennedy, I hate you like I hate a rattler. I hate Jackson like I'd hate the lowest thing on earth. Johns, yo're just a filthy, unwashed pawnbroker that handles the things left by murdered men. You, Brady, I don't want to kill you, even if you do need it. When I do, I'll give you an even break. There's my cards, spread out plenty wide."

"Plenty wide," said Kid Brady, "is right, Stroud. I'll say this much for you: you got nerve. More nerve than any man I ever knowed, except Ike. When the time comes, mister, for you and me to play fireworks, you'll git an even break. And you kin tie into my pop an' chewin' gum any time. It ain't often a man meets a gent that's game enough to make a play like you made."

"Shut up, Kid," growled Kennedy, "or I'll put you in the pen, where you belong. The pen I got you out of. I pay you ten times what you're worth, and you act like a fool. Shut up. Stay shut up. Double-cross me and you'll hang."

Ike Babcock took a stick of the Kid's gum. Their eyes met in a swift glance.

Luther Johns pocketed the four hundred dollars. His

one eye was a bloodshot slit.

"You've preached your own funeral sermon, Stroud," he said. "Only fools talk. I'm taking the four hundred dollars as interest on what you owe me. Interest on twenty-five thousand that I lost. No man ever outfoxed me. A man carved out my eye once. I collected with a knife. When I finished my whittling, his own mother wouldn't have known him. I'm going down now to open the store. I buy, sell, or trade for anything. But I've never yet lost out in any kind of a trade. Steep on that, Tom Stroud." The gangling, one-eyed, stoop-shouldered Luther Johns left the room.

"Time we were on our way, Kid," growled Kennedy. "Let's git out of this hole."

Ike Babcock and Tom Stroud were left alone. The big, homely cowman looked at Tom, who still stood there, the white-handled gun in his hand. Ike Babcock shook his head.

"Kinda overbet yore hand, didn't yuh, Tom?"

After helping himself to another piece of steak, Ike Babcock looked across the campfire at Tom Stroud. It was nearly midnight.

"Only a plumb locoed idiot would 'a' done it, Tom."

"Mebbeso yo're right, Ike. But layin' in behind a bush or a rock ain't my style. I had to tell 'em. Luther Johns knows it was me that took that money. Jackson had a strong hunch it was me that run off the cattle you delivered to him. They had 'er made to kill me the night I went with you an' Cassidy an' Chick. So I played the game open, Ike. I played it the way I like it."

"They're after yore scalp, Tom."

"And I'm after theirs."

"Why?"

"If I live to tell the story, Ike, you'll know it."

They were camped down below the border. The cowboys were drifting into camp from their spree at Cayuse. Some were drunk. Some were sober. Some were broke. Others had more than they had started in with. But these latter cowboys were few.

Most of them carried bundles of clean clothes tied to their saddles. Some among them had got a shave and haircut, and where the hair had been sheared or shaved off, the skin was oddly white in contrast to their bronzed skin.

"For all the world," said Ike Babcock, "like a bunch o' pintos. Look at 'em."

The Mexican barber at Cayuse had been deft with the clippers. And he had been overgenerous with cheap hair tonic and talcum.

"Look at 'em," said Ike Babcock. "Now, take Pete, there. That hair-shearin' Mex like to run outta hair when he fixed Pete up. Pete's gal will run him off the place with them curly locks gone an' his head showin' all them knots an' knobs. She'll no doubt run him off with a skillet."

The cowboy named Pete grinned sheepishly. "I kinda dozed off in the barber chair, Ike. But I shore smell good."

"Yeah. Yuh shore smell purty. Git off to the windward."

Someone of the Mexicans was playing a guitar. The stars hung low in the sky. The firelight threw red lights and shadows across the faces of the men. A coyote sang his song to the moon.

A cowboy was telling a story about outlaws and cattle and horses that had carried men through danger.

"Biggest liar this side o' Peace River in Canada," said

Ike Babcock.

Another cowboy was rapping the trail dust from a harmonica, his eyes red for lack of sleep.

One or two were bedded down. Some others had spread out a sweaty saddle blanket and were playing poker with a deck of cards that was service worn with long handling.

"Like it, Tom?" asked Ike Babcock, drinking black coffee and eating Dutch-oven biscuits. "I shore hate to leave it, Ike."

"Leave it?"

"I laid out my cards too plain, Ike. No use draggin' you into it. Them gents of the Cayuse Cattle Pool has my name on their black book. I'm goin' after 'em like I told 'em I would. You stay outta the game, Ike. I'm playin' 'r lone-handed."

"We'll talk that over at the ranch, Tom."

"Better fire me right now, Ike."

"I got no reason to fire you. Shucks, I got no use for King Kennedy or Jackson or Luther Johns. Kid Brady is all right, except that he'd rather git in a gunfight than go to a dance. Which reminds me, there's goin' to be a fiesta at the ranch. A padre is comin' to baptize some kids and marry off some o' the vaqueros to their best girls. You wouldn't want to miss that. It'll last a week, I reckon. Then, after the fiesta, we'll declare war on the Cayuse Cattle Pool. You an' me. I've been intendin' to do it for a long time. Now let's lay 'em down. I see you bought a bed off Luther Johns."

"You know the bed?" asked Tom, as he laid back the tarp.

Ike Babcock pointed to the Lazy S brand on it. "Yeah. It belonged to a kid cowboy. I forgit his name now. He worked for me a few weeks, then pulled out.

He hired out to the Cross X outfit. Got killed in a gunfight. Jackson killed him. The young cowboy didn't have much chance, I reckon, against Jackson an' Luther Johns. They make a bad team. Nope, I bet that cowboy never had a fightin' chance. Not against the Jack o' Spades an' them white-handled guns Luther packs. He was a good boy, as I recollect him. A tow-headed, blue-eyed button that was a good hand any place you put 'im. I hated to see him leave. But he wanted to see more country. He had some money on him and a good outfit. His private saddle horse an' pack horse was likely lookin' geldin's. Seems like his name was Jones or Smith or some common name." His puckered eyes were watching Tom.

They crawled under their blankets. The music of the guitar and harmonica had stopped. The yarn-spinners had gone to bed. The camp-fire was now but a bed of coals, graying.

Tom Stroud lay between blankets that were stained with the blood of a young cowboy who had been murdered by Jackson and Luther Johns. Tired as he was, sleep would not come to Tom Stroud. He lay there on his back, watching the stars, watching the moon in a cloudless sky. And he was thinking of the young cowboy whose bed he now owned.

SMOKE MEN

SIESTA! TOM STROUD, in his room at the old rancho, shaved and bathed. The bath was quite a performance. Tom stood outside while two Indian servants threw bucketsful of water on him. Warm, then cold—cold as ice. He rubbed down with a coarse towel. He had slept twelve hours, between white sheets, in a room that was set apart for the special guests. It was about seven-thirty in the morning.

Tom's boots had been shined. Clean clothes lay on the bed. Outside he could hear the slosh of water as another guest got his bath. The bather was laughing and singing in the Mexican tongue. An Indian *mozo* brought in a basket of fruit.

"To eat while you dress, señor."

"Who's the singin' gent?" Tom asked, then repeated the question in the Mexican tongue.

"That is Colonel Ruiz, señor."

"Ruiz? Colonel Ruiz?" Tom Stroud grinned and helped himself to an orange. "The bandit?"

"To us, señor, he is no bandit. He is the great leader of the cause. Some day he will be in power. That will be a happy day for the oppressed. He is a great man. He is a defender of the poor."

"I've heard of him many times."

"He is the friend of the Señor Babcock, my *patron.*"

Tom dressed. He went outside. Ike Babcock was sitting on the porch, eating breakfast. He grinned and motioned Tom to a chair at the hand-made table.

"Order what you want, Tom. Ham and eggs, beefsteak, anything. Sleep good?"

"Like a rock, Ike."

"Good. You won't git much sleep tonight, I bet. There's a hundred or more good-lookin' señoritas to dance with. Plenty of *vino* to drink. Good music. No fights. I reckon you'll enter in the ropin' and ridin' and bulldoggin'?"

"Shore thing."

"You'll have hard competition, Tom. Set down."

A portly, genial, brown-robed padre joined them. But

he did not order breakfast.

"He can't eat till he says Mass," explained Ike. "And if ever a man liked his grub, it's the padre. Here comes the colonel."

Colonel Ruiz, in the garb of a vaquero, joined them. After the introductions, he ordered a hearty breakfast.

"Then you are not going to confession and Communion this morning, Colonel?" asked the Padre.

"Tomorrow, perhaps, or the next day. After I have attended to certain matters. We have some duties to attend to, Señor Padre. They are most urgent. After that— *Salude!*" He lifted his glass of yellow orange juice.

"The colonel took some prisoners last night, Padre," said Ike Babcock. "They need his attention."

Tom Stroud understood. There would be a bullet-pocked adobe wall. Men lined up. A firing squad. That was Mexico. He saw the troubled look in the brown eyes of the fat padre.

"There is no other way?" asked the priest.

"No other way, Señor Padre," replied the bearded rebel. "They are traitors to the cause."

The fat padre turned to Ike Babcock.

"Mass will be delayed. Tell the people. Señor Colonel, I go with you. There will be those who will welcome the words of a priest."

"It is a long, hard ride from here, Señor Padre."

"I am accustomed to long, hard rides. Perhaps, before we reach your camp, I shall be able to intercede for those unfortunate men. Perhaps I may be able to save their lives."

"Remember," said Ike Babcock, "it's fiesta time, Colonel. After all, they learned their lesson, I reckon. They'll not double-cross any man again.

"You wish, then, that I let them live?"

"Punish them some way, Colonel. Enough to drive home the lesson. They'll make good soldiers."

"But do you understand, my friend, that there are vaqueros in your employ that are the guilty ones? They are traitors to you."

"Fetch 'em here to me. I'll put 'em haulin' wood an' buildin' a new barn I need."

They carried on a conversation that was a mixture of Spanish and English, slipping glibly from one tongue to the other. Colonel Ruiz smiled and nodded.

"Ees like you weesh, señor. You and the Señor Padre are too soft of heart. I warn you, my friends, some day you weel learn that the only way to handle these men ees to handle them weeth the gun. Where would I be eef I got a softness of the heart? Pouff! Dead like the rocks. But thees morning I must also get thees softness of the heart. I send a man to have the prisoners brought here. And the fiesta shall go on. '*Sta bueno.* Now I must change to my best clothes. There is one among the señoritas who pleases the eye of a caballero. Tonight I shall sing the songs of Old Mother Mexico beneath her window. After all, it is better to sing love songs than to shoot prisoners, no?"

He got to his feet, bowed, and left them. Spurs jingling, he went away, humming. The portly padre turned to Ike Babcock.

"Thank you, señor. In that chapel you have rebuilt I baptized that hot-tempered caballero. Perhaps, at the same altar, I shall unite him in marriage to some señorita. I dread that day when I must bury him beneath this blood-spattered soil of my Mexico. Señor Babcock, today you have saved men from death. May God bless you for your generosity. I shall remember you in the

Mass. Now I must go."

The old chapel bells were ringing. Tom and Ike, there in the shade of the vine-covered arcade, watched the men and women and children, all in their best clothes, going into the church. The brown-robed padre, his silver hair shining in the morning sunlight, was among them, chatting, smiling, shaking hands, patting small black heads.

Now Colonel Ruiz, resplendent in his fiesta clothes, joined the throng. Ike Babcock smiled at Tom.

"Who are the men, Ike, that he took?"

"Some gents that was layin' in a canyon to kill us when we come back from Cayuse. Jackson had bought 'em off with *tequila* an' *marijuana* an' a few dollars. Ain't them bells purty music?"

"Purty music, all right. What'll you do with 'em, Ike, when you git 'em?"

"The bells?" Ike gulped his coffee.

"Them prisoners."

"Hard to say. I ain't sayin', Tom. Depends on who they are. I'll look 'em over. Ruiz says they're bad hombres. He knows his own kind better than we do."

"Supposin' they're bad?"

"I'll turn 'em back to Ruiz after the fiesta. There's no use messin' up the fun with a firin' squad. After the padre pulls his freight, after the big fiesta is over, I'll take care o' them gents. They'll git a fair trial. Them as looks and acts straight will git a new deal. Ruiz will take care o' the others. And the padre won't never know the difference. This is Mexico, an' if a man is goin' to stay alive down here, he's got to *sabe* things. You'll learn the *sabe* of it after a while, mebbe. If you don't, they'll git you."

Ike got to his feet and hitched up his overalls.

"We might as well go on down to the church, Tom. Can't hurt a man none."

"I don't mind, Ike. Say, what's that yonder? Looks like smoke on that pinnacle."

Ike Babcock jerked his hat down across his head with an abrupt pull. His hand moved the gun, in his low-tied holster. His grin was not mirthful. His eyes were hard.

"Come on, Tom. Church'll have to wait. Trouble acomin' down the trail." He called to an Indian *mozo.*

"Tell Colonel Ruiz to come along up the main trail with a dozen men. Tell him to slip outta church so's the padre won't know. Tell the major-domo to have every man ready."

"What do you expect, Ike?" asked Tom.

"Can't tell yet. That smoke sign means trouble. It might be ten men or it might be a army."

Tom followed him to the barn. They saddled up, shoved carbines in the saddle scabbards, and left the rancho at a long lope.

Ike Babcock led the way, keeping clear of the main trail. Tom followed him, wondering what was going to happen. The smoke signal, on the pinnacle several miles northward, no longer was visible. The course which Ike Babcock was picking twisted and doubled back through the heavy brush. Cat's-claw and mesquite raked their clothes. Sometimes they were blocked by a heavy wall of manzanita which they would have to go around. They had gone some distance when Ike Babcock drew up, pulling his Winchester from its scabbard. He dismounted. Tom followed suit. They crawled through a dense thicket. From where they crouched they had a view of the main trail, not fifty feet distant.

Someone on horseback was coming along the trail, coming at reckless speed.

"Sounds like one rider, Ike."

"He's shore scratchin' dirt gittin' here, whoever he is. I wonder if— Yonder he is."

A cowboy on a big, sweat-marked sorrel burst into view. Ike Babcock hailed him.

"What's the rush, cowboy? Where's the fight?"

"That you, Ike?" The man pulled up.

Ike motioned Tom to stay hidden. The big cattleman stepped out on to the trail, his carbine in his hands.

"What's the smoke about?"

"Company a-comin', Ike."

"Who are they?"

"Two border patrol men. Feller named Cassidy. His pardner's called Chick."

"They're all right. They can't hurt nobody down here. You orter know that. The United States law ain't got a foot to stand on down in Mexico. They're welcome. You boys take them badges too serious. Pass 'em on along the trail. Tell 'em how to git to the ranch. There's a fiesta goin' on down there."

"That ain't the half of it, Ike. There's been trouble."

"What kind o' trouble, feller?"

"Three o' the boys on guard last night pulled out, runnin' off the extra horses. They knifed the nighthawk. That left me an' another boy on guard at the pinnacle all night. Him and me was on first guard. We never got relieved. Stayed on all night. Come daylight I rides down to camp. Nobody there. No horses in the corral. No fire. Then I finds the nighthawk dead. Yo're out three men and fifteen head o' horses."

"We'll git 'em back. Ruiz will pick up the men an' the horses. I'll send up men an' horses from the ranch to guard the trail. You an' yore pardner hang an' rattle till they git there. Go back an' pass the two border patrol men down the trail."

"An' supposin' them three gents, mebbe more, that run off last night, take a notion to come back, Ike?"

"Do I have to tell you what to do? I pay you twice what any man is worth. You got guns and ca'tridges to fit them guns. What do you think you hired out for?"

"You mean to—"

"I mean to play yore string out or else rabbit on me like they done. If yo're scared, say so, an' I'll pay you off."

"I ain't scared, Ike. Only one o' them three fellers that pulled out last night is my kid brother."

"I don't care if he's yore great-grandmother. You take my orders or git off that horse."

"I'll keep on workin', Ike. Only I hate to have harm come to the kid. When we left home down in Texas, I promised the old man I'd kind o' look after the button. I—"

"Go on to the ranch. Draw yore time. Then head back for Texas an' go back pickin' cotton. That's where you belong. Git outta my sight before I set you afoot an' make you walk back to yore cotton patch. I don't want yallerbacks like you. Git goin'."

"But Ike, I said I—"

"Pull yore freight. Go to the ranch. Stay there till I show up. Git outta my sight!"

The cowboy went on down the trail. Rejoined Tom. The big cowman forced a grin.

"They come beggin' jobs, then lay down when trouble starts. Tom, you wait here for the colonel. Come on with them. I'll go to meet Cassidy."

"You ain't goin' along, Ike. Somehow that gent's talk didn't sound right. He didn't tell it all."

"Think he lied?"

"He didn't tell all he knowed, Ike, that's all."

"How do you mean, Tom?"

"If my hunch is right, there's a trap laid for somebody. You or me or somebody. I'm goin' along."

"All right, Tom. Let's git goin'."

LAW OF ESCAPE

IT WAS CALLED Smoke Signal Pass. A boulder-strewn trail where only one man could ride at a time. Its granite pinnacle marked a corner of Ike Babcock's land grant. There was a wider, more traveled route that was used when trailing cattle up out of Mexico. This was, as it were, a secret pass, cutting off many miles, and only used by men who were the good friends of Ike Babcock. Ike had always kept a guard there. Five men. Five men, at Smoke Signal Pass, could hold back an army, providing they had guns and ammunition.

"Look out, Tom!"

Ike Babcock quit his horse, his gun spitting fire. Tom needed no warning. He was on the ground, carbine in hand, crouched among the boulders along the trail. Their horses, excited by the gunfire, took to the brush as rifles cracked.

Tom and Ike Babcock squatted in behind the granite rocks. Ike grinned widely.

"You made the right guess, Tom. It's a trap."

Bullets kicked bits of granite over their heads. They flattened themselves on the ground, taking an occasional snap-shot at one of the dozen or more men who were throwing hot lead their way.

"Hit that un in the laig," said Ike Babcock, shoving fresh cartridges into his short-barrelled saddle gun. "We should 'a' set that Texas liar afoot, Tom. You shore had the right hunch. Let them coyotes have all you got."

"I'll do my best, Ike. Who do you reckon we're shootin' at?"

"Hard to tell. Mebbeso it's fellers after Ruiz's scalp, wantin' to git down to the ranch. Mebbe it's them dope runners. They been quiet about just long enough to bust out. It might be the Cayuse Cattle Pool after my hide. Kennedy wants my ranch down here. He's tried every way he knows to git it."

"Or it might be the Cayuse Cattle Pool comin' after me," said Tom. "Hope I ain't let you in for trouble, Ike. You should 'a' let me go on back from the first night's camp."

"I need you, Tom. I been expectin' trouble. There's some crooked politicians down here that Kennedy has been dickerin' with. The only thing that keeps 'em from confiscatin' my ranch is Colonel Ruiz and a man in Mexico who stands ace-high with the *presidente.* Kennedy is most likely behind— You asked for it, amigo!"

As he spat out the last words, he pulled the trigger of his carbine. Over in a brush patch a man threshed around on the ground, cursing, groaning. Ike jerked the lever of his carbine.

They were badly outnumbered. But the big boulders made an excellent barricade.

"Shoot to cripple 'em, Tom."

Tom nodded and jerked his gun trigger. A man gave a hoarse cry of pain.

"That'll fix his shoulder for a while, Ike."

"Me an' yore dad fought Injuns together once, Tom. Did he ever tell you about the time we got shut in like this? Him an' me. A handful o' ca'tridges. No water. No grub. There must 'a' been fifty Injuns. We held 'em off two days an' nights. Tom got a arrow through his thigh an' a bullet-hole in his shoulder. But he never made a whimper. Not once. He was shore game."

"He told me," said Tom, "how you patched him up and packed him through the night, dodgin' Injuns. How you saved his life. He told that story many a time to me and Davy."

"Davy? Who is— I remember now. Davy was the baby. I mind hearin'—"

"Hearin' how he was arrested for rustlin' a couple o' years ago, down along the border. Davy was mixed up with a bad crowd. But he was a good boy. Watch that black rock yonder, Ike. There's a feller. Don't shoot!" And he knocked Ike's gun barrel upward just in time.

Now Ike Babcock, his face a little white, looked at the man who was leaning against the black boulder in an awkward, unnatural position. The man's arms were tied behind him.

"It's—it's Cassidy!" whispered Ike.

"They shoved him in sight, hopin' he'd stop a bullet," growled Tom Stroud. "There's blood on his face. He's groggy, Ike. They wanted us to kill him. It didn't work."

"It come almost workin'," said Ike Babcock grimly, as he ejected a smoking shell from his carbine. "Thanks, Tom. You got keen eyes. I had my sights lined."

"How'd they git Cassidy?"

"The same way they got us caught in the fly paper, Tom. Some slick trick. And it smells like the Cayuse Cattle Pool."

Now a white rag was waving at the end of a gun barrel. It was Cassidy's partner, Chick. Chick, standing out in the open. He looked weary and haggard.

"What do they want, Chick?" called Ike Babcock.

"They want you, Ike. There's about twenty men here. They grabbed Cassidy and me as we came through the pass. Some of 'em are Mex. Some of 'em are your own men. Some are Kennedy men. Never mind what they do to us, Ike; wipe out this nest of rattlers. They're holding Cassidy and me prisoners, hoping to get ransom money. They want ten thousand dollars in cash. They say they'll quit shooting at you two men if you'll send ten thousand cash by the man you met on the trail. That's to pay ransom on Cassidy and me. Don't pay it! Kill 'em off. Slip back to the ranch and bring men. Wipe 'em out. Never mind me or Cassidy. It's all in the game, Ike. You savvy how—"

Chick was jerked out of sight. Ike and Tom could hear him cursing his captors.

"They had a rope around Chick's neck," said Ike. "Jerked him off his feet when he talked the wrong words. Game gent, that Chick feller. The same goes for Cassidy. Set easy, Tom. Squat low an' roll a smoke. Because in a little while— Duck! What did I tell you? Warfare is done declared!"

From all around them came the sound of cracking rifles. Men on horseback, others on foot. A short, swift, bloody fight while it lasted.

Then, up near the black rock, Colonel Ruiz, on a black horse, lifted his hat and waved it.

Ike Babcock stepped out from behind the rocks. He stood on a granite boulder and waved his hat.

"Come on, Tom. The show's over. Them boneheads should 'a' knowed better than to try a trick like that. I knowed that Ruiz, when he heard the shootin', would surround them would-be tough gents and kind o' deal 'em misery. I hope Cassidy an' Chick didn't git killed."

"Listen, Ike, you knowed all along that the smoke

signal was a trap."

"Shore thing, Tom. I set a trap for the gents that set this trap. Put men I was leery of, there on guard. Left word with 'em that I'd be wantin' to go alone to Cayuse an' when the trail was clear, to light the smoke signal. Knowin', all the time, that they'd lay a trap."

"So you had Ruiz foller with his men?"

"Yep. He was in on the scheme I'd fixed. There was men in his outfit he couldn't trust. I had my men I couldn't trust. Kennedy had bought 'em. Ruiz knowed how to surround them gents."

"But why did you want to go ahead alone, leavin' me behind to wait for Ruiz? Ike, Ruiz was here before we got here. He had 'em surrounded when we come up the trail. You wanted to leave me outta the fight, ain't that the idea?"

"Somethin' like that, Tom. Me an' you took a sort o' crooked trail. Ruiz an' his boys slipped up by a short cut that only a dozen men in all Mexico know. He had 'em corralled when we rode up. It was him that fired over our heads to warn us. Tom, it's a great game, this game I'm playin'. More fun than a three-ring circus."

"I don't savvy it, Ike."

"You will, before long. Let's see what damage was done. I never tell any man too much. But when you been down here a spell, you'll see things an' hear things. An' a man that can't figger out what he sees an' hears ain't worth botherin' with. Every man that works for me is watched. No man kin double-cross me an' come out lucky. Yonder comes the colonel. He's got Cassidy an' Chick with him.

There was a wry smile on Cassidy's tanned face. His head was bandaged. His hands were tied behind him, as were Chick's.

"Nice, pleasant trip to that fiesta of yours, Babcock," he said grimly.

"You was comin' to the fiesta, Cassidy?"

"Not exactly. I was coming down to have a talk with you. That was a neat trick you slipped over on me about delivering those cattle. And this reception is a pretty rough welcome. What are you going to do with Chick and me?"

Ike Babcock took out his pocket-knife and cut the ropes that bound the two law officers.

"So you figgered I'd laid this trap for you, Cassidy? Go ask one o' them wounded men what it's about. Yo're free to go back to the border, Cassidy, an' I'll furnish you with a bodyguard. Or you kin come on down to the ranch. Yo're welcome, you an' Chick. But git this through yore head, mister. Ike Babcock don't play underhanded. I'll outfox you on a cattle deal, mebbe. But I don't bushwhack men. If you want to see what is goin' to become o' the men that trapped you, hang around a spell. Eh, *compadre?*" He grinned at Colonel Ruiz.

"It weel geeve me the great extreme pleasure, amigo, to show thees officer of the United States how men of Mexico deal weeth traitors." He stroked his black beard, white teeth flashing.

"This is Mexico, Cassidy. And I want you to shake hands with the gent that saved yore life. Colonel Ruiz."

Cassidy's eyes narrowed. "Colonel Ruiz?"

"*Si, señor.* You 'ave hear of me, perhaps?"

"And if it hadn't been for him, Cassidy, you an' Chick would be eatin' supper on yonder side o' the big divide. So would me an' Tom, here. An' while yo're bein' thankful, Cassidy, take a look at Tom Stroud. He knocked my gun barrel up just in time when them murderin' devils shoved you out by that black rock."

"What kind of a game are we playing?" asked Cassidy. "What's it all about?"

"Ask us no questions, Cassidy, an' you'll hear no lies. Colonel, we better keep them prisoners on ice. Have the boys hold 'em back in the hills. Any news from up the trail?"

Colonel Ruiz spoke rapidly in Spanish. His dark eyes were flashing, his hands moving expressively.

"Old Farias is dead. The horses have been run off from the rancho where he lived. He fought well, that old one, but one of your gringos tricked him. Farias was shot in the back. He forgot to keep his back to the wall when he held them off with his gun."

"You know the gringo, *compadre?*"

"*Si*. He is one of the prisoners."

"Tom," said Ike Babcock, "you know the trail back to the ranch. If Cassidy an' Chick still want to go on to the ranch, pilot 'em down there. How about it, Cassidy?"

"Thanks, Babcock. We'll—call the bet."

"You will be my guests, savvy? Yo're goin' as my friends. This is fiesta week. Tom, take care of 'em till I git home."

"All right, Ike."

"The major-domo will show 'em their room. See that they git the best. Tell the padre we went out after stray cattle or somethin'. Don't let on about what happened. He will feel better if he don't know. Kids to baptize, lovers to git married. Prayers to say for the dead. Handle him right, Tom."

Tom Stroud nodded. "I'll take care o' him, Ike."

"Then hit the trail with Cassidy an' Chick." Ike turned to Colonel Ruiz.

"Give that murderin' gringo a six-shooter an' a horse

an' turn him loose, pardner. Tell the men not to bother him."

"*Ley del fuego?*"

"Yeah. *Ley del fuego.* Law of escape. I'll handle his case, personal." Ike Babcock shoved fresh cartridges into the cylinder of his six-gun. His puckered eyes were hard as glass.

Church bells, older than the oldest man in Mexico, calling their summons in the velvet dusk. Vespers. Ike Babcock was letting Tom Stroud care for a slight bullet wound in his thigh.

"Plenty o' that iodine, Tom. A snake's bullet might pack poison. You like the fiesta?"

"I'm havin' as good a time as ever a man had, Ike."

"Church bells an' blood. Red wine an' guns. They sing an' they cry. They laugh an' they kill. In the end they die. Pull that bandage tighter, Tom. That's it. How's Cassidy an' Chick makin' er?"

"They're havin' a good time, Ike."

"They'll git the savvy of it after it's all over with. They're safer here than if they was in jail. Hope this laig won't keep me from swingin' them gals aroun' this evenin'. Now if it had been my head, the bullet would o' glanced off."

Ike Babcock pulled on his new overalls, turned them up at the bottom, and shoved his feet into a pair of shop-made boots. Then he put on his shirt and struggled with a tie.

"Need help?" Tom grinned.

"Are you hoorawin' yore boss? Listen, Tom. I had me a set o' good ties once. Bought a dozen of 'em. They fastened with a hoodus in back. Saved a man all this work. If I couldn't tie a steer in faster time than I tie one o' these bow ties, I'd— Tom, tie 'er up some way. I'm licked."

He held up his hands. Tom managed to get Ike's black bow tie tied.

"I had one on one night, goin' to a dance about twenty-thirty miles from here. Come a rain. The sweatband or whatever you call 'er on this tie commences shrinkin'. I cut 'er off just in time to keep from chokin' to death. I give the rest o' them ties away to cowboys that was tryin' to beat my time with this yaller-haired schoolmarm I was courtin'. Then come a three-year drought. No rain. Them sons wore out the ties, an' one of 'em married the yaller-haired gal. Not one o' them suckers choked down."

From somewhere came the sound of a man singing. The splashing of water. Ike Babcock grinned widely.

"That's Ruiz, back. He's a game cuss, Tom. Game as any man I ever knowed. I'd like to see him made governor."

Tom did not ask where Colonel Ruiz had been, or what he had been doing. But he knew that the rebel Ruiz had taken some prisoners to a hidden camp in the hills.

Tom asked Ike no questions concerning the bullet wound in his thigh. He knew of the Mexican law, *Ley del fuego.* The law of fire. The law of escape. Only, in this instance, the prisoner had been given a loaded gun and a horse. And somewhere Ike Babcock had caught up with the man. And the murder of old Farias had been avenged. No need of questions. Ike Babcock never welcomed questions.

Presently Colonel Ruiz joined them. Again he was resplendent in his fiesta raiment. Sharp contrast to the homely, overalls-clad Ike Babcock. Seldom did Ike ever wear anything but overalls. But he had made Tom put on a suit of store clothes that he dragged out of a huge closet. In the closet were suits, uniforms, hats. All sizes. All well-tailored. The hats were new, of the best beaver. That was Ike Babcock's way.

Cassidy came in.

"They told me you'd gotten back, Babcock. Thought I'd drop around to see you."

"Take a chair, Cassidy. There's liquor, wine, whisky, brandy, anything you want, in the sideboard. Cigars an' cigarettes. Even *marijuana* cigarettes that I keep on hand for Luther Johns. Got everything you need? They treatin' you all right?"

"No kick coming on that score."

"Chick gittin' along good?"

"Some señorita has him in tow. He's dancing his head off. Hope he don't get married and stay down here."

"Then everything is all right." Ike Babcock grinned.

"Not quite. I want to talk to you alone."

"Then come into the other room. Tom, you an' the colonel wait for me here."

In the next room, Ike Babcock faced Cassidy. "Well, what's on yore mind, Cassidy?"

"*Ley del fuego.*"

Ike Babcock's eyes hardened. "Better forget it, mister."

"While they held Chick and me prisoner there at the pass, Babcock, I heard some talking. Some of it in English, some in Mex. The talk had to do with an old Mexican named Farias. There was a big, black-haired Texican who was half drunk. He boasted how he had gotten this Farias. He said he had fought him in the open, in a fair fight. He said—"

"He lied, Cassidy."

"Whose word are you taking?"

"The word of a man that don't lie. Go ahead with yore song an' dance. Cut yore pigeon wing. Keep talkin'."

"This Farias kept a way station for smugglers. He kept horses and grub and guns and ammunition there. Is that right?"

"Plenty right, so far as the grub an' horses an' guns are concerned, Cassidy."

"You don't deny it, then?"

"Farias has worked for me for a good many years. The guns he kept there belonged to me. The horses wore my brand. The grub was beans an' my beef an' chili peppers he raised. Go ahead, Cassidy."

"You admit all this, Babcock?"

"Why' not? It ain't no secret in Mexico that ol' Farias worked for me."

"And you'll admit that you smuggled in guns and smuggled out whisky?"

"Shore thing." Ike grinned and scratched his head. "Shore, I run guns. I run booze. I run wet cattle acrost the line. You don't need no magnifyin' glass to find that out. Ask any o' the old heads along this part o' the border. I been playin' checkers with them boys for a long time. Is that all you got to say, Cassidy?"

"Farias worked for you then."

"Shore thing. And a finer old feller never drawed breath. He'll be buried here in a day or two. He was a good friend to me. As good a friend as a man could ask for. Go ahead, Cassidy. What else on yore mind or is that all?"

"No, it's not all, Babcock. Not by a long shot. You admit to me that you run guns and booze and handle wet cattle. You admit that this old Farias worked for you. That right, Babcock?"

"I said so, once. Ain't that enough?"

"Farias was killed. That right?"

"Shot in the back. Murdered."

"We won't go into that right now. Farias was killed. He died fighting, I suppose?"

"He got four men before that skunk murdered him from behind, if that's what you mean."

"And the man who killed him was a big Texican with black eyes and black hair, with a knife scar on his face and two fingers gone from his left hand. That right?"

"That's the polecat, Cassidy."

"Where is that man now?"

"Hold on, Cassidy, hold on. Yo're kinda gittin' yore laigs all twisted, steppin' ahead o' yorese'f. I'll ask you one now. Just what is it to you where this gent is?"

"I'm not here to answer your questions, Babcock. I'm questioning you."

"I savvy. Go ahead." Ike Babcock's voice was a slow, unhurried drawl, but his eyes were narrowed, cold.

"Where is the man who killed Farias?"

"Not bein' in touch with things outside o' this world, Cassidy, I can't say. But I'd bet all I got, down to my last smoke, that the big son ain't in heaven."

"He's dead?"

"What if he is, Cassidy?"

"You killed him. And I'll take you back on a John Doe warrant for murder."

"I didn't know you was one o' these practical jokers, Cassidy. Yore warrant ain't no good in Mexico."

"It's backed by the government of Mexico, Babcock. Get your hat, and we'll go. You're under arrest."

Ike Babcock chuckled. "You and me have been talkin' here alone, Cassidy. In any court, my word is as good as yourn. What I've said to you, no man has heard."

Cassidy smiled thinly. He stepped to a closet door and pulled it open. His jaw dropped in dismay. Ike's brief laugh straightened him.

"Lookin' for Chick, Cassidy? You'll find him locked in the cellar where we keep the hawg corn. Seems like Tom Stroud ketched him slippin' in here, hidin' in the closet. Tom taken care o' him. Tom's handy, that a way. That's why I hired him. Set down, Cassidy. Yo're goin' to listen to me."

WAR DECLARED

NIGHT CLOSED IN SLOWLY, with purple shadows that became black. There was a round moon and yellow stars that were like specks of gold. There was the music of guitars. The laughter of beautiful señoritas. The soft lullaby of a Mexican mother who nursed her baby which had been baptized that day.

Candles lighted in the chapel. The odor of incense, there in the place of humble worship, and in the open air, the unmistakable odor of talcum powder and perfume.

The brown-robed padre and his beads, there in the candlelight. Out yonder the fiesta where the more worldly pleasures held sway. On his knees the padre prayed for the soul of Farias. Out yonder, where the red wine spilled into thirsty throats, men pledged vengeance. During his life, old Farias had made many friends. He was not without them now, even after death.

"Take'er easy, Cassidy, an' listen." Ike Babcock jerked loose his tie with an impatient gesture. His eyes, clear, steady, watched the law officer. "Set down."

Cassidy sat down. The big cattleman tossed him a package of gum.

"Chaw on that, mister. Do you good."

"So I lose the deal, Babcock?"

"You never had the deal, Cassidy."

"I thought I had all the aces."

"Just a bob-tailed flush, Cassidy. Directly, I'll have Tom turn Chick loose. There's a sayin' in Mexico, but I reckon you never heard it. It says to a guest: 'Enter your house.' Cassidy, you busted the unwritten law o' hospitality down here. But I'm not countin' it because you thought you was doin' yore duty. Arrest me? Arrest Ike Babcock in Mexico? Ask any man you talk to how far you'd git.

"Cassidy, I'm tryin' to save you an' the Chick feller from bein' hurt. You boys has been workin' over in California. This ain't *Baja California.* This is a bronco State in Mexico. Them hills out yonder hold men that 'ud kill you for a peso. Chaw that gum an' think 'er over. Tonight is fiesta night. I'm goin' to dance till sunrise. You kin join in. Hear that music? Hear them folks havin' a good time? They're my guests. They're my friends. All of 'em liked ol' Farias. Hang around a day or so an' you'll learn somethin' about this neck o' the wild country. Take off yore badge an' gun an' leave 'em here in the house. Git out there an' have a good time."

"Babcock, I can't do a—"

Ike Babcock's laugh filled the room. He slapped the border patrol officer on the back.

"No hard feelin's. Git out there an' join in the fun, Cassidy. If you want me to go back next week, I'll go along. You won't need no bench warrant."

Cassidy looked at the big, homely cowman. Ike did a

jig step and picked up his tie from the floor.

"Tie this dad-burned thing, Cassidy. Kin you tie a bow knot that'll hold?"

Cassidy held the tie in his hand. Ike buttoned the collar of his shirt.

"I can't figure you, Babcock."

"Don't try. Just set yore mind on that fool bow tie. Make a good job of it because I'm shinin' up to my best gal this evenin'. Behave, an' I'll give you a knock-down to her. Now git busy with that tie. They're waitin' for me out yonder."

Cassidy tied Ike Babcock's tie. He had to reach upward. Ike leaned his head backward. Finally the task was finished. It was as if the knotting of that bow tie was Ike Babcock's greatest worry.

"It's tied," said Cassidy.

"I'm obliged."

"Babcock, you make me feel like a six-year-old kid. I— Here's my gun and badge. I'm going to give—"

"Shore thing, Cassidy. We'll git Chick outta that corn cellar. Dress him up an' turn him loose out yonder. Yo're all right, mister. You got nerve. Some day you'll savvy. Let's git out yonder an' swing them gals aroun' to the tune o' that music."

"Babcock, I've acted like a low-down coyote. I can see it that way now. I figured I was smart. But I'm not. I betrayed a trust. It won't happen again."

"Forgit it, Cassidy."

Tom Stroud shoved his head inside the door he opened without bothering to knock.

"You got company, Ike."

"Meanin' just who?"

"The main ramrods o' the Cayuse Cattle Pool."

King Kennedy, big, florid, stood there in the

lamplight in the living-room. He was helping himself to a drink of whisky. Luther Johns was hunting in the sideboard for *tequila.* Jackson, who hadn't taken off his chaps or spurs, leaned against the wall, watching Colonel Ruiz. Kid Brady, whistling through his teeth, was hunting for gum.

Ike Babcock greeted them with a chuckle that became a laugh. He poked Cassidy in the ribs.

"The fiesta is drawin' plenty folks." He turned to Tom Stroud. Behind Ike Babcock's grin was a hardness that was the hardness of steel. It showed now in his eyes.

"Tom, take care o' the Chick gent. See that he gits whatever he wants. Tell him that Cassidy and him is special guests. And tell him to have a good time. Take Cassidy along."

When Tom had gone, Ike Babcock turned to King Kennedy. Ike's eyes were narrowed a little.

"Did you come for the fiesta, Kennedy, or did you come here huntin' trouble?"

"Neither, Babcock."

"Then what fetched you here?"

King Kennedy shrugged his heavy shoulders and poured himself another drink.

"We were on our way to the State capital when we were stopped and fetched here by yore men."

"Kinda taken you by su'prise, I reckon?"

"Yeah." Kennedy's voice was gruff.

"Where did they pick you up, Kennedy?"

"Smoke Signal Pass," said Kid Brady.

"And since when has the trail to the State capital led through Smoke Signal Pass?" asked Ike Babcock.

"A man has a right to pick his own route, Babcock."

"Shore thing, Kennedy. And my men has orders to

fetch in every man that comes through the pass."

King Kennedy glared at Colonel Ruiz. The Mexican rebel stroked his black beard and said nothing.

"There were over fifty Mexicans in the gang that stopped us, Babcock. What's the game?"

"Always, Señor Kennedy," said Colonel Ruiz, "my soldiers have orders to assist the men working for my good friend, Ike Babcock. They seen everyone who comes across the border. Just a precaution. The wolf must watch for the hounds, no?"

"How long are we to be held here, Babcock?" growled King Kennedy. "When do we go?"

"You kin go tomorrow, I reckon, unless somethin' turns up to hold you here."

"Prisoners, are we?" said Luther Johns.

"Not exactly. Yo're stayin' over for a funeral. We're buryin' my old friend Farias tomorrow. I figgered you'd like to stay over for the funeral. Then Colonel Ruiz will give you a military escort to a place in the mountains. Some friends o' yourn are up there. They're goin' to be lined up an' shot, accordin' to a ol' Mexican custom. I want you gents to see the show."

"Babcock," snarled Kennedy, "you ain't winnin' so much as a white chip on this deal."

"Mebbe not, Kennedy, but I'm bettin' plenty."

"How you fixed for red pop?" asked Kid Brady.

"Shut up," snapped Kennedy. "Learn to keep that big mouth of yours shut."

"You shore are in a bad humor," returned Kid Brady. "Yesterday, when we started down, you was as good-natured as ol' Santy Claus. Singin' an' whistlin'. But after we git stopped at Smoke Signal Pass, you been like a bear that's turned over a bee nest. I'm just askin' Ike for some red pop. And I'm about outta chewin' gum,

Ike."

"I'll fix you up, Kid."

"Look here," growled Kennedy, "are you workin' for me or Ike Babcock, Kid? I got a notion to fire you right now."

"You'll git another notion," said Kid Brady, "that'll beat that first un. Fire me and see how long it'll be till some hombre fills you full o' bullets."

"Supposin'," said Ike Babcock, "that we cut out this sparrin' around and git down to cases. You talkin' turkey, Kennedy?"

King Kennedy looked at Luther Johns, who had just lighted one of his *marijuana* cigarettes.

"Keep your mouth shut, King," advised Johns.

"Then I'll talk some," said Ike Babcock. "I'll talk and I want every man of you to listen."

"Going in for speech-making?" Luther Johns smiled.

"Tomorrow," said Ike Babcock, "my old friend Farias fills a grave. He's got a heap o' friends here. Friends that 'ud make 'er kind o' hard on them that had him murdered. Them same friends would likewise make 'er tough aplenty for any man that had ideas about wipin' me out here in Mexico. Hear that, you gents?"

"How about the red pop, Ike?"

"Look in the cooler in the next room, Kid."

"Go on with the story," said Luther Johns.

"Smoke that thing outside," said Ike, "or else put it out. If you gotta smoke *marijuana,* smoke it where it won't smell up a man's house."

Luther Johns pinched out the lighted cigarette and tossed it out through the doorway. His one eye glittered, and his scarred face was a malignant mask.

"Go ahead with the story, Ike," he said.

"You sent yore men out to clear the pass, Kennedy.

They kind o' fell down on the job. You been playin' politics down here. You want this ranch o' mine. Well, you ain't gittin' it. You'll see of Farias buried tomorrow. One word from me an' the men that are the friends o' that of man will shoot you down in yore snaky tracks. Hear that?"

"Continue," said Luther Johns.

"You'll see yore murderin' skunks shot down by a firin' squad. Got that straight?"

"Perfectly," said Luther Johns.

"Then," Ike Babcock finished, "you kin go yore way."

"You mean that?" asked Kennedy.

"I told you so. I don't lie. Not even to men like you an' Luther Johns an' Jackson, Kennedy."

King Kennedy gulped his drink.

"Think this will win you anything, Babcock?" he asked.

"Dunno, Kennedy."

"Babcock, you ain't got a chance in a million. I got you where I want you. I got Ruiz where I want him. I got Tom Stroud where I want him. You'll all get it where the turkey got the axe. I've got every last one of you over a barrel."

Ike Babcock grinned at Colonel Ruiz. The Mexican bandit smiled and stroked his black beard.

"I never knew before, Kennedy, that you was comical, that a way, makin' jokes."

"In ten days this ranch will belong to me, hear that?" barked Kennedy.

"Mebbeso. Most mebbe, not. *Quién sabe?* Who knows? Bet a hat I don't lose 'er, Kennedy."

Kid Brady came in with a bottle of red pop. He looked at Ike Babcock, and if the others had been watching, they would have seen Kid Brady make a small, almost imperceptible gesture, with the open bottle of pop.

"I located it, Ike," said Kid Brady.

"Figgered you would, Kid."

Kid Brady cocked his head to one side, listening to the music. His grin widened.

"How's chances to join the fiesta, Ike?"

"Yo're welcome. So is everybody. You kin use Tom's room to shave in an' git fixed up. Kennedy, you an' Luther an' Jackson kin take the same room you always use."

He clapped his hands, and an Indian *mozo* showed in the doorway. Ike spoke to him in his native tongue.

"Show these men to their rooms."

When Ike Babcock was alone with Colonel Ruiz, his face settled into grave lines.

"Well, amigo?" he asked.

"News has come in, *compadre,*" replied Colonel Ruiz, "that Señor Kennedy has used his political friends down here in Mexico, to gain his ends."

"That means," said Ike Babcock, fumbling with his bow tie, "that we have to work harder to gather cattle, no?" He spoke in Spanish. Ruiz lighted a cigarette.

"Worse than that, *compadre.*"

"What do you mean?"

Colonel Ruiz took some papers from his pocket and spread them out on the table.

"These were taken from a messenger who was to meet Kennedy. Look them over."

Ike Babcock read the papers. His lips tightened in a wry smile. He looked at Ruiz.

"They've sold me out, eh? Those dirty *politicos* who played with Kennedy have cancelled my grant down here. Wiped me out. Busted me. That's why Kennedy was so almighty sure o' hisse'f. That's why Luther Johns grinned like a buzzard. Buzzards don't grin, *compadre,* but if they did, they'd look like Luther Johns. Has Kennedy seen these papers yet! Does he know he's got my ranch?"

"Not yet, my friend. And if you say so, he will never know. You are my one great friend in all the world. You have been more than kind to my people. You have cared for them when they were sick. You have fed them when they were hungry. You have given education to their children. You have won their love and their loyalty. You have rebuilt this old hacienda. I, who was born in this very house, have always found a welcome here. It is like coming home to visit with a brother when I come here.

"*Compadre,* that gringo Kennedy has it in his power now to ruin all this which you have so carefully built. He will put in his cursed gringo thieves. They will tramp on the floors where my mother walked, carrying me, a baby, in her arms. They will tear down the pictures, the images of the saints. They will spill their whisky on the tiled floor of the old chapel. They will pull down those old church bells. They will take what they really want and trample on what they don't desire.

"*Compadre,* let me finish them. Let them take their places among those other traitors who will be shot!"

Ike Babcock shook his head. "Take a drink of wine, my friend. And forget Kennedy. I'll handle that big cuss. They'll go to the funeral tomorrow when old Farias is buried. Then they'll go along and watch some friends of theirs get their dose of lead poison. And when they come back to the ranch, I'll hand over these papers to Kennedy and send him on his way."

“And lose the rancho?”

“Lose nothin’, pardner,” said Ike Babcock. “From tonight on, we fight. This is our ranch, an’ we’ll hold it.”

“You mean that you—”

“I mean we’ve done declared our war, old pardner. Out in the open. Win, lose or draw, we’re fightin’. Git word to the State capital that we’ve done declared ourse’ves!”

FIESTA NIGHT

IKE BABCOCK ROLLED A smoke and grinned at Colonel Ruiz. “Pardner, will you tie this tie o’ mine? Cassidy is a good law officer, I reckon, but he shore can’t build a bow tie. It come undone on me. Now you tie ’er hard an’ fast.”

“Hold the ’ead back, *compadre.*”

“I’m holdin’ ’er back.”

“The Adam apple, ees jomp up an’ down when you talk.”

“All right. I’ll keep my trap shut. Have at ’er.”

Colonel Ruiz placed Ike Babcock in a chair. He maneuvered the big, raw-boned cowman into a semi-prone position.

“Don’t put a knee under my briskit, Ruiz. An’ don’t shave me nor jerk out my teeth while you got me down this a way. I’m a hound fer punishment, but I’d hate to kill off a good—”

“How many times do I tell you to quit talking? Every time I tie the tie for you, I— *Compadre,* that apple of Adam jomp like the jomping jack on the steeck!”

“You like to choke me down.”

"I do the best I can weeth— Hold quiet!"

Ike Babcock sputtered, coughed, choked, then lay back in the big chair.

"Try once more. I'll lay quiet."

"Per'aps eef I knock you on the 'ead?"

"I'm all right now. Had me a jawful o' the Kid's gum. Swallered it."

Colonel Ruiz, when he laughed, laughed like a boy. His dark eyes danced with merriment. Finally the tie was fixed. For a moment, those two men who had, so many times, looked at death, had forgotten the danger, the almost inevitable death that awaited them in a few days, a week, a month, perhaps.

"Tonight we dance, Ike."

"I'll tell a man."

"And mañana?"

"Tomorrow, pardner, we bury ol' Farias."

"And the gringos?"

"Will stick around till the fiesta is done. They'll git all they bargained for, before they're done."

"*Bueno.*"

"Yep. *Bueno. 'Sta bueno.* Very good."

Their glasses touched. They drank their wine in silence. Then, together, they joined the crowd that was dancing outside under the moon. Dancing on worn tiles made by hand by the Indians.

Torches lighted the huge patio. Bright-colored dresses. Scarlet. Yellow. Pink. Emerald-green. Sombre black here and there, denoting mourning. The tinkle of silver-mounted spurs. The soft strumming of guitars. The laughter of women. Fiesta.

Tom Stroud laid a hand on Cassidy's shoulder. "No hard feelin's, Cassidy?"

"None, Stroud."

"I squared myse'f with Chick. He was sorta ringy at first, but I joshed him out of it."

"And got him a good-looking girl to dance with."

"You bet. Better limber up yore laigs, Cassidy. Which girl do you want to dance with?"

Kid Brady came up. He was wearing a pink silk shirt and a red tie, and his hair was slicked down with water.

"Know where I kin git a dance, Stroud?"

"I'll see what I kin do, Kid. Gosh you look like a mornin' glory just busted into bloom."

"Taller in my boots an' a pair o' store pants," said Kid Brady. "Even had a bath an' shave. I'm rearin' to go."

"Heeled?"

"Ain't sayin', Stroud. You needn't worry, feller. I worked here long enough to know the rules. I ain't bustin' no caps. I'm as peaceable as a lamb."

Tom turned him over to a Mexican vaquero. "Kid Brady's feet is itchin' to dance. Look after him, Juan."

"You fit in down here, don't you, Stroud?" said Cassidy, looking hard at Tom.

"Yeah. Why not? I'm roddin' Ike's spread."

"I owe you a debt, Stroud. I'd like to pay it off, in a measure. I want to tell you something."

"Shoot it, Cassidy."

"Get out of here. Quit Mexico."

"I reckon you wasn't listenin' close when I said I was ramroddin' Ike Babcock's outfit."

"Ike Babcock can't last long. He's in with Ruiz, and they're both in bad with the Mexican government."

"I reckon Ike kin hold his own, Cassidy, an' Colonel Ruiz acts like he wasn't a weaklin'."

"They're finished in Mexico. I got it from Luther Johns a few minutes ago. Johns is drunk, and he talked.

King Kennedy has bought this old ranch. They'll wipe out Ruiz. They'll get Babcock if he stays. Pass that on to Ike Babcock."

Cassidy walked away. Tom's gaze followed him. Then Tom walked back to the house and went inside.

But Ike was not there. Nor was Ruiz. Tom found Ike at the barbecue pit, laughing and joking with a crowd.

"Kin I see you alone, Ike?"

"No law agin' it, Tom."

Back in the shadows, Tom repeated what Cassidy had told him. Ike Babcock nodded.

"Any time, Tom, that you want to pull out, you know where to find yore horse. You know the trail back to where you come from. You kin saddle up any time."

"Who said I was saddlin' up, Ike?"

"Cassidy said a heap. Me an' Ruiz has just a fightin' chance."

"Then I'll split that fightin' chance with you, Ike."

King Kennedy and Jackson looked at one another as they washed last night's cobwebs away with cold water.

"Seen anything of Luther?" asked Kennedy.

"He's asleep."

"Where's the Kid?"

"He's playin' stud poker with some o' Ike's cowboys."

"And Ike wants us to go to this funeral this mornin'?"

"So he said. Looks like we ain't got much choice, King."

"Then we'll go. Jack, have you learned what become of the tough gent that we hired to rub out Farias?"

"He's dead."

"You plumb sure?"

"Plumb. Ike handled the deal."

"Personal?"

"Personal, King. Ike thought a lot o' Farias."

"Ike Babcock is diggin' his own grave," growled Kennedy, as he shaved.

"Him and Stroud."

"And Ruiz," added Kennedy.

"And Ruiz."

"Jack," Kennedy wiped the spots of lather from his face, "I don't trust Kid Brady. He likes Babcock a lot."

"And you want him taken care of, King?"

King Kennedy nodded. He picked up his trousers and reached into a hidden pocket.

"They took our guns away from us at the Smoke Signal Pass, Jackson. But they didn't know I had this small un hid in my pants. Only one man knowed. I had that gun. That man is Kid Brady. Here's the derringer pistol. Git the Kid in the right spot an' let him have both barrels. He'll not be watchin' you."

"How much, King?"

"Five hundred."

"No kin do. Make it a thousand and wipe off my debt on them stampeded cattle, and I'll git Kid Brady and Stroud to boot."

King Kennedy helped himself to a drink. His pale eyes watched Jackson. Then he shook his head.

"I'll do the job myself. No man kin rob me like you're tryin' to rob me, Jackson."

"Think it over, King."

"Are you scared o' Kid Brady?" growled Kennedy.

"No, but you are. The Kid knows you got that gun. He's faster than you when it comes to gun play. Make one false break, and he'll kill you, King. Think'er over."

"The Kid ain't heeled, Jack."

"The Kid is heeled. Babcock staked him to a gun last

night. There was a six-shooter in there where the Kid got his red pop. He's packin' a gun, and he's handy with it. How about my price?"

"Yo're lyin', Jackson."

"Am I? Wait till we go to breakfast. Kinda brush up against the Kid an' accidentally on purpose lay a hand on his left flank. The Kid is left-handed, ain't he? Well, you'll feel a hard bulge under his coat on his left flank. Mebbe it's a bottle o' red pop. But I got a notion that it's a six-gun.

King Kennedy scowled at his reflection in the mirror. He was not pleased with the puffy pouches under his eyes. His face felt hot, flushed, in spite of the cold water he had used on it. His hands were puffy, a little shaky, too thick for quick work. Too slow with a gun when he went up against a fast gun thrower like Kid Brady. And he knew that Kid Brady would be watching him. He spoke, watching Jackson's reflection in the mirror.

"You're askin' a big price, Jack. I've done a lot for you, here and there."

"And I've done a few things for you, King, that no other man would do. You laid me out for spillin' that herd. I taken it then because I had to take it. But I don't have to take it now. This is Mexico. We're prisoners, you might say, here at Ike Babcock's ranch. Supposin' I was to git drunk and talk some. Say I told Ike that you give that Texican two hundred dollars to kill Farias? What if I let it out that you hired men away from Babcock and Ruiz and promised 'em money if they'd do some good shootin'?"

"You mean you'd squeal on me, Jackson?"

"Squeal? Not me. But when a man is drunk, he's apt to talk too much. And I'm gittin' drunk today."

Kennedy turned around slowly. The little derringer

was in his hand. His eyes were congested with hatred.

"Jackson, I got a mind to shoot you."

Jackson stepped from behind the bed. There was a thin smile on his lipless mouth. In his right hand was a cocked six-gun.

"If I was in yore place, King, I'd put away that cap pistol. It ain't loaded."

King Kennedy's heavily jowled face became a flabby, mottled mask. His dry tongue passed across his heavy lips.

"You mean that—"

"That I fixed that popgun a few nights ago when you was drunk and asleep. Kid Brady let it slip that you packed that little pistol. And figurin' that some day you might turn on me, I slipped blank shells in the gun. I got two good cartridges that will fit that gun, King. But they will cost you a few cents. You got me workin' off the price o' them cattle. Cancel that debt and you'll git two real cartridges for yore gun. Pay me a thousand on top o' that, and I'll take care o' Kid Brady and Tom Stroud. Do we talk the same language?"

King Kennedy's hands were shaking. He knew Jackson. He knew that the cocked gun in Jackson's hand meant business. Last night's dissipation had shattered the big cattleman's nerves. And he had the sense to know that Jackson, sometimes known as the Jack of Spades, was not in the habit of bluffing.

"You got me, Jackson. Got me acrost a barrel. Don't shoot. I'll wipe the slate clean and give you a thousand dollars. Give me the two cartridges for the pistol."

"Here they are, King." Jackson tossed the two .44 rim-fire cartridges on the dresser. "Fork over the thousand."

THE LOCKED CABIN

OLD FARIAS WAS BURIED in the old graveyard behind the chapel. Women in black. The deep, soft voice of the padre. Here and there a woman's low sobbing. Stern-faced men.

More than one pair of eyes looked hard at Kennedy and Jackson and Luther Johns and Kid Brady. News travels fast in Mexico. And it was being whispered that these men of the Cayuse Cattle Pool had something to do with the old Mexican's murder.

"I don't like the way these greasers are acting," Kennedy told Jackson.

"Me neither. But there's nothin' we kin do about it. We're here. Can't make a get-away."

"If you'd taken my advice," muttered Luther Johns sourly, "we wouldn't be here. I told you to wait till we got the papers and some soldiers to back the play. But no, you had to send out a gang of yellow-backed fools to clear the trail. And here we are. Not even a gun among us if they jump us. I saw a Mexican wearing my two white-handled guns. We're in a tight spot."

When the funeral was over, Ike Babcock, Colonel Ruiz, and Tom Stroud went back to the house. Ike summoned an Indian *mozo*.

"Tell the gringos standing down by the winery to come here at once."

Kennedy, followed by the others, came into the living-room. Luther Johns made a bee line for the sideboard.

"Hold on, mister," said Ike. "Stay away from there. You gents are on the Injun list. No more booze. Not if yore tongues are hangin' out a foot. There's a strong jail here on the place. If any of you is ketched tryin' to git a drink or a bottle, you'll go in that jail. If I was you gents, I'd go into your room an' bar the door. Old Farias left a lot o' friends behind. Yo're stayin' here a week. Try to make a get-away, and my men have orders to shoot you.

"This afternoon there's goin' to be a bullfight. The bull is about eight years old, lean and tough. After he's killed, we're butcherin' him. You'll live on bull meat. I hope you all got good teeth. There's a stove in where I'm puttin' you. You'll do yore own cookin'. There's beans that I'd aimed to th'ow out because they ain't much good. I reckon you'll find weevils in the flour. The coffee is the kind we give to the peons. There ain't ary beds or beddin', so you kin sleep on the dirt floor. I hope you don't mind rats.

"There won't be no lamp or candles, so you might as well bed down with the chickens. No more fiesta for you gents, I reckon. You seen them women in black? Them's the old feller's kinfolks. Daughters an' nieces an' so on. The men with 'em is their husbands an' brothers an' uncles an' such. Kennedy, they all thought a heap o' of Farias. Now, if I was in yore fix, gents, I'd lock myse'f in that cabin an' stay there." He turned to Tom Stroud:

"Show 'em the cabin, will you, Tom?" He walked over to Kennedy:

"Git outta here, Kennedy, or I'll throw you out!"

Tom pointed out a small adobe cabin. It was at the edge of the Mexican quarters.

"There's yore castle, gents. Head for it. I'll foller behind a ways so's you won't be bothered."

They went in silence. The crowd of Mexicans standing around eyed them as they walked past.

"I reckon, Kennedy," said Tom as he ushered them into the small, dark adobe cabin, "that Ike must 'a' forgot to tell you that Ruiz has put off executin' them friends o' yourn until after the fiesta is over. Well, in you go. Don't git lonesome."

Tom went to the barn where he found Ike Babcock. Ike was saddling his horse. A score or more of cowboys and Mexican vaqueros were roping and saddling horses at the corral. They were laughing and joking.

"Bet a hat, Tom, that I beat yore time in the steer tyin'," said Ike.

"Call it, Ike."

"Too bad them Cayuse Cattle Pool gents won't git to see the contests this week. All of 'em but Kid Brady will be havin' shakes before many hours. And they'll be locked in that cabin. It has a patent lock that kin only be opened from the outside. The bars on the window is plenty strong. And wait till Luther Johns tackles that bull meat with them snaggle teeth o' his. Luther's goin' to be the worst off. Ever see *a marijuana* smoker when he's cutoff from his hop? He goes plumb loco. He'd kill his own mother for a smoke."

"Ike, I got a notion that Kid Brady has a gun."

Ike jerked his latigo and knotted it, then looked at Tom. There was a queer grin on his face.

"Yeah, the Kid has a gun. I staked him to a gun and a box o' shells when he got here. King Kennedy likewise has a gun. A little two-barreled derringer pistol Jackson was slick enough to buy off some Mexican. And unless I'm plumb stupid, Luther Johns has managed for some kind of a smoke pole by now. If they git to janglin' among their se'ves they all got guns."

"If I was to bet another hat," said Tom Stroud, "I bet you let Kennedy keep that pistol a-purpose. I'd bet you fixed that Mexican to sell Jackson a six-shooter. And I bet you know where and how Luther Johns got holt of a equalizer."

Ike Babcock unhooked his stirrup from the saddle horn, then took his service-worn chaps from a peg and buckled them on. He stepped up on his pet rope horse and grinned down at Tom.

"Bet a hat I beat yore time for three calves, Tom." And he rode out to join his men.

Tom mounted his horse and followed Ike. He wondered just what would happen in that locked cabin when three men, half-crazy from want of liquor to ease their shattered nerves, would turn on one another. And he wondered just what kind of a man this big, homely, grinning, raw-boned Ike Babcock was anyway.

Tom Stroud won the steer roping. Ike Babcock beat his time tying down three calves. The big cowman grinned at his foreman, as he said:

"No hats won, Tom. No hats lost. Looks like we'll have to git along with these same sky-pieces. Well, yonder goes the bull meat for the Cayuse Cattle Pool. Jackson's brag was that he never ate his own beef. Well, he'd orter enjoy that bull."

Tom Stroud unsaddled his horse. He had been thrown in the bronc riding, and his face was skinned across one side.

"I bet even a hound dog wouldn't eat that meat, Ike."

"I wouldn't ask my dogs to tackle it, Tom. Dog-gone, that was some rodeo. Colonel Ruiz shore looked like ten million dollars headin' the big parade. Tom, you still bettin' hats?"

"On them guns?"

"Nope. Forget them guns packed by the Cayuse Cattle Pool. You got a one-track mind."

Tom grinned faintly and wiped the blood and sweat and dirt from his skinned face.

"Name the bet, Ike."

"Bet a hat that Colonel Ruiz is the next governor of this State in Mexico."

"You heard any news, Ike? Inside information from the City of Mexico?"

"Nothin', Tom. I'm playin' a hunch, that's all."

"I'll call the bet."

"And I'll bet another hat that King Kennedy never owns this ranch down in Mexico."

Tom unbuckled his chaps and shoved his six-gun into the waistband of his overalls.

"I ain't callin' that un, Ike. I don't reckon Kennedy will live long enough to grow a week's worth o' whiskers."

"Mebbe yo're right, Tom. How's yore face feel?"

"As raw as that bull meat you just sent over to the Cayuse Cattle Pool. Outside o' that, it feels like the same face I been usin' for a long time."

"You shore lit on yore head. There's a lump the size of a goose aig there above yore ear. You'll have a hard time makin' a hit at the *baile* tonight when the fiddles start playin'."

"If I'd lit on my feet, I might 'a' busted both laigs. As it was, I just peeled off some hide an' got a little sleep."

"You was out half an hour, feller. Thought you'd never come alive. Tom, if I was you, I wouldn't pack all that money around on me. There's enough in that money belt o' yourn to tempt even an honest man. Better put it in my safe."

"How did you know I had—"

"I told you you was out, cold. Yore shirt was half tore off. You wasn't breathin' so good, an' I kinda loosed up yore Levis. I wasn't snoopin', Tom. Nobody but me an' Ruiz seen it."

"It's what I took from Luther Johns and Kennedy, Ike. It goes to some folks *they* robbed. Some widows and kids down in Texas. You kin keep it in the safe."

Ike Babcock nodded. "It'll be all right there."

They went to the house to clean up and change clothes. It was sunset, and the crowd was gathering around the barbecue pits. Campfires were being lighted.

In his room, Tom Stroud undressed. He had given his filled money belt into Ike Babcock's keeping. He peeled off his torn flannel shirt. His head felt dizzy and splitting with pain. That bronc had piled him hard. His neck had been badly wrenched, almost broken by the fall. He was lame and bruised and still a little bewildered from the shock. Now he stood there, in his undershirt and overalls, a queer look in his eyes that were bloodshot from dust and sun. His hands felt down across his undershirt. He pulled off his boots and shook his dusty overalls.

There came a rap at the door, and Tom's hand closed over the butt of his .45 that lay on the dresser.

"Come in," Tom called.

The man who came in, shutting the door behind him, was Cassidy. Tom, naked save for his underclothes, laid his gun back on the dresser. He grinned a little sheepishly.

"Take a chair, Cassidy. I'll be with you as soon as I git a few buckets o' water th'owed on me. What's good for a headache?"

"If that question came from some people, for instance certain members of the Cayuse Cattle Pool, I'd prescribe a little of the hair of the dog that bit you. But, in your case, some good liniment rubbed where it will do the most good along your neck and shoulders, and aspirin. I brought both. Get your bath, and I'll see what we can do. That was a nasty fall, Tom."

"You ain't tellin' me no fresh news. Have a cigar or a drink or somethin'. And I'll join you in a jiffy."

The crude bath felt good. Hot water, then cold. Tom gave the wooden-face *mozo* a dollar and dried himself with a rough towel. Then he went back inside. From the outside "bath" next door Tom could hear Colonel Ruiz singing.

Cassidy had taken off his coat and rolled up his sleeves. On the dresser he had put bottles and jars of liniment and salve.

"I got the stuff from Babcock's store," explained the officer. "I had two years in medical college. It comes in handy."

"It's good of you, Cassidy, to drop in."

"Nothing else to do."

"How's Chick?"

"He's eating this evening with the family of a young lady who calls him 'Cheekie.' He's got it bad."

Cassidy began rubbing Tom's neck. His hands were strong, capable, skillful. The pain was being rubbed away.

"What's on yore mind, Cassidy?" asked Tom when the job was done and he was dressing.

"What makes you think there's something on my mind?"

"Just a hunch. You made one or two mistakes down along this part o' the border, but yo're learnin' fast. Yep, learnin' plenty fast, I reckon. Nobody that knows the border ever accused Captain Pat Cassidy o' the border patrol of bein' dumb."

"And nobody ever accused—"

Tom cut in quickly. "All right, Cassidy. You win. I wondered when you'd remember me."

"I didn't peg you till today."

"You told anybody?"

"No."

"Not even Chick?"

"Not even Chick."

"Good. Now what do we say to each other?"

"Stroud, what's going to happen here? What's going to happen to Kennedy and the men with him? They're locked up in that place. Luther Johns is acting like a madman. Kennedy is roaring like a mad bull. That man Jackson sits in a corner, never opening his mouth. Kid Brady chews gum and plays mumble-peg. Something will happen in that cabin tonight."

"That's Ike's business, Cassidy. This is Mexico. This is Ike Babcock's ranch."

"And in that cabin are four American citizens. Crooks, I grant you, but nevertheless they're Americans."

"Gringos, down here, Cassidy."

"Kennedy has money. He's a power."

"If I was you, I'd not lose much sleep about Kennedy. I reckon Ike is just joshin' 'em some."

"Murder is no joke, Stroud."

"No." Tom Stroud pulled on his boots. "You said 'er that time, Cassidy. Murder ain't a joke!"

"Then let's make Ike Babcock stop that damnable torture he's inflicting on those men."

Tom selected a clean shirt. Cassidy was pacing the floor. One of his boots squeaked.

"Better grease that boot. It squalls like a panther, Cassidy. And light a cigar."

"Look here, Stroud, this is no time for fooling.

There'll be murder done in that cabin."

"Let 'em hop to it. It'll save the law a lot o' trouble and money. They're all bad. All of 'em need killin'. Let 'em fight 'er out then. Let 'em start shootin'."

"But, listen, man, they are citizens of—"

"They're border renegades, Cassidy. Take yore troubles to Ike, or the padre. This is Mexico, not California."

A GOLD BADGE

IT WAS DUSK WHEN Tom Stroud found Ike Babcock at the barbecue pits. Ike was eating with a bunch of cowboys. Tom called him to one side, out of earshot.

"Ike, I'm worryin' about them gents inside the locked cabin. I listened outside. Kennedy and Luther Johns were cussin' one another. There'll be trouble in there before mornin'."

"Wouldn't be su'prised, Tom."

"All but the Kid are hard drinkers. They're needin' liquor right now worse than a starvin' man needs grub. Luther Johns is half loco now. Hadn't we better give 'em a jug an' slip Luther Johns some of his doped cigarettes?"

"We'll walk over there, Tom. Come on."

Ike led Tom to the one small window in the cabin. Inside, there in the darkness, could be heard the mad cursing of Luther Johns. And King Kennedy's surly growling.

"How you makin' 'er, boys?" called Ike Babcock, cautioning Tom to stand behind him. They were against the outside wall, invisible to the men within.

"What's your price, Babcock?" snarled Luther Johns.

"Name your price and let me out."

"Don't git so impatient, Luther. Yo're in good company. You boys kin kinda git confidential. Swap stories and so on. Luther, you might begin by tellin' King Kennedy how, all the time, you was double-crossin' him. Buyin' whisky from me dirt cheap an' makin' Kennedy pay three—four prices for it. Tell him how you been sellin' me an' Ruiz guns an' ammunition when you knowed all the time that Kennedy had put a price on the head o' Colonel Ruiz. You made plenty o' money on the side, Luther. I kept track of it on my books. It runs into six figgers. Tell King that story. It'll soothe him down."

"You lie, Babcock!" snarled Luther Johns, his voice harsh. "You lie. He's lying, Kennedy."

"I got proof of it all at the house. Receipts signed by you, in yore own handwritin', Luther. When I let you gents outta here in a week, I'll prove what I say."

"Listen, Ike," whispered Tom, "yo're makin' things worse in there, talkin' that a way. Don't do it."

"It's my show, Tom, I'll run 'er." He raised his voice again.

"Jackson, you might he'p along King Kennedy's temper some when you tell him how you been buyin' wet cattle from me on the side and havin' a third party sell 'em to Kennedy at a big profit to you. Tell him how drunk you was the night them cattle was spilled. Tell him how you've let plenty o' them dogies drift back into Mexico, hair-branded, and I'd pick 'em up an' sell 'em back, an' we'd split the profits. That'd make a good story for King to listen to while he's feelin' kinda bad. It'd shore cheer him up."

"Ike, what in Sam Hill you tryin' to do?" muttered Tom.

"Just ribbin' up a little talkin' bee to amuse 'em in there. Now let's go over to where the dancin' is."

"Not yet, Ike." Tom's gun poked Ike Babcock in the back. "I want the key to that cabin, Ike. Those men in there need hangin', but that's plain torture. I want that key."

Ike stood there, his hands above his head. When he spoke, there was more amusement than anger in his voice.

"I keep the key locked in the safe, Tom. If you feel that way about it, let's go to the house an' git it. Let 'em loose, if you like. Turn 'em loose. They can't git off the ranch, an' them kinfolks Farias left behind will take care of 'em. No hard feelin's, Tom. Let's go git the key. You kin turn 'em loose."

Ike Babcock lowered his arms, grinning at Tom. Then he led the way to the house.

"It ain't that I want 'em turned plumb loose, Ike," said Tom, following the big cattleman through the dusk. "But they're sufferin' in there. They need liquor, and Luther Johns needs his dope. Now they'll be fightin' in there like crazy men. Ike, I don't want to be actin' like this, but—"

Ike's hearty laugh came back out of the dusk. "I told you, Tom, no hard feelin's."

Tom felt uneasy. Ike Babcock could torture men as he was torturing those men of the Cayuse Cattle Pool. And he could laugh and dance without a thought of the suffering he was causing those men.

Then there was something else that was worrying Tom Stroud. His left hand passed across the breast of his shirt. He scowled a little, and the grip on his gun tightened. Ike Babcock was a dangerous man. Gun runner, whisky smuggler, cattle thief. He had tricked an old-timer like Cassidy, made Cassidy and Chick look like schoolboys on a Boy Scout outing. What would he do if he suspected Tom Stroud's game? What if Ike had found—

Ike whistled the tune of "Sam Bass" as he led the way into the house. Tom followed him into the room he used as an office. Ike, still whistling somewhat tunelessly, began working the combination of the huge safe. Tom, his hand on his gun, stood in the open doorway.

"Reach high, Stroud!" snapped a voice behind him.

Tom whirled, crouching. Three men were covering him. His hands lifted slowly. Ike took Tom's gun and laid it on top of the safe. He grinned widely.

"That's all, boys. Tom was just foolin'. He's still ramroddin' my outfit. He and me had a bet a hat that he could git the drop on me. I'm owin' him a hat. That's all. You boys kin go. Tom, how about a little nip? In the front room."

He slapped Tom on the back and pushed him, none too gently, out of the office. The three cowboys clumped out, looking at one another with puzzled glances.

"Set down, Tom. That was a horse on you, feller."

Tom took a chair. He grinned faintly.

"It's a horse on me, Ike. Well, what are you goin' to do to me?"

"I'm goin' to take you over to the *baile* an' introduce you to some good-lookin' girls. You heard me tell them boys o' mine that you was still ramroddin' the outfit, didn't you? You young fellers take things too almighty serious. Before we go over to the *baile*, I want you to git somethin' through yore head, son. It takes a smart man to fool ol' Ike Babcock. Especially when he's on his home ranch. Here's how. Now grin. It's me that has that

hat comin'. One hat you owe me. Drink hearty."

When they had tossed off their small glasses of old brandy, Ike Babcock walked into the office, motioning Tom to follow him.

He handed Tom his six-gun.

"Somethin' might come up and you might need that cannon," he said.

Then, turning his back to Tom, he worked the combination of the big safe and swung open the door. Still squatting on his heels, he reached into his pocket and brought out a gold badge—the badge of a Texas Ranger.

"I taken it off yore undershirt, Tom, when that horse th'owed you. We better lock it up in here with yore money. It'll be safe. There's some o' these gents at the fiesta that ain't losin' no love on law officers. Nobody but me an' Ruiz knows."

Again turning his back, Ike put the badge in the safe and closed the heavy door.

"Now, Tom, let's git to that *baile*. Hear that music?"

"Ike, I don't know what to think. I come from Texas for a reason."

"To git the man that killed yore daddy. And to git the man that killed yore kid brother that night in Cayuse. You told me you believed me when I said I never killed yore dad. I don't think yo're a liar. If I didn't trust you, son, you'd be locked in with them gents o' the Cayuse Cattle Pool. Yore badge won't do you no good down here in Mexico. It might mean trouble for you. You kin have it back when you leave here, providin' we git a chance to leave."

"What do you mean, Ike?"

"Keep yore eyes open an' yore mouth shut. Ask me no questions, an' I'll tell you no lies. Now let's git to that dance. My feet's itchin'."

So Ike Babcock knew that Tom Stroud was a Ranger. He knew that Tom had come to find his father's murderer. He knew that the young cowboy who had been killed in Cayuse was Tom's younger brother. And he knew that Tom Stroud, Texas Ranger, was on a special job to wipe out the Cayuse Cattle Pool and put a stop to Ike Babcock's dealings along the border.

How long would it be before big Ike Babcock would wipe the genial grin off his homely face and hand Tom over to the men who hated all law officers? What if he knew that Tom was planning to grab Jackson, Kennedy, Luther Johns, and Kid Brady and, with the assistance of Cassidy and Chick, rush them back across the border and into the hands of the United States law? Did Ike Babcock know that there were men waiting at the border now to take charge of the members of the Cayuse Cattle Pool?

In talking to Cassidy, who had recognized him as a Texas Ranger, Tom had talked one thing, then practised another. He knew that Cassidy and Chick were being constantly watched. That their conversation was probably being overheard, there in Tom's room. So he had played a part. And now he wanted to locate Cassidy. Cassidy and Chick. But they were not at the *baile*.

Ike was dancing one dance after another, laughing, cracking jokes, having a good time. Now and then he would take Tom over and introduce him to some dark-eyed señorita. Tom kept dancing. He felt that he was being watched all the time.

Ike had told him to keep his eyes open and his mouth shut. This he was doing. And he kept his ears open, likewise.

The Mexican orchestra kept playing. Dancers kept dancing. But there was a noticeable scarcity of men. Most of the men were cowboys. Only a thin sprinkling of the men from the hills who claimed Colonel Ruiz for their leader. And there was no sign of Ruiz.

Tom watched the faces of the men and women. They danced, they smiled, but behind their smiles lay a nervous tension. They seemed to be waiting, watching for something, someone. They gathered in whispering groups between dances. Of them all, Ike Babcock was the only person who seemed carefree.

Another thing. Every man there was armed. There was little wine flowing. Just enough to quench the thirst of the dancers.

At the chapel candles burned, and a brown-robed padre prayed. In the chapel were women, all in black. Now and then a girl in fiesta dress would drop in and pray. They were mostly brides of yesterday. Tonight their husbands were not there at the *baile*.

Tom Stroud noticed these things. There was trouble coming. Trouble of some sort.

"You shore danced the slippers off that last señorita, Tom," said Ike Babcock, mopping his perspiring face with a big silk handkerchief. "Havin' a good time?"

"Can't holler, Ike."

"Kep' yore eyes open?"

"Some."

"What did you notice?"

"Plenty, Ike. There's trouble a-comin'."

"For a man with one guess, you shore hit the bull's eye. It's comin' from down below. Soldiers aplenty. Ruiz has gone to meet 'em. We expect a ruckus tomorrow or next day. The Kennedy *politicos* down here ain't takin' my ranch without a fight. We're fixin' to handle ’em. So you better git in what dancin’ you kin tonight, Tom. Because mebbeso tomorrow you go back acrost the border into the old U.S.A.”

“What about Cassidy and Chick?”

“They go with you, I reckon. I had to put ’em under guard, Tom. Cassidy was puttin’ up a holler about them Cayuse Cattle Pool gents. I knowed him and Chick would git in trouble if they tried to spring them snakes outta the cabin, so I had ’em put in the house. They got plenty to eat an’ drink. Books to read. A phonograph to play. Tobacco. But it wouldn’t do to let ’em loose tonight.”

“What becomes o’ the Kennedy layout, Ike?”

“Not knowin’, couldn’t say. It all depends on the next few hours. They’re shore gittin’ snaky. All but the Kid. I got a guard aroun’ the cabin. Don’t leave the *baile,* Tom. I figger I’ll be needin’ you before long.”

“Ike, I ain’t goin’ back without Jackson an’ Kennedy. Jackson killed my kid brother, an’ I’m goin’ to see him hung. Either that or I’m killin’ him, personal. And I got enough on Kennedy to send him up for life.”

“How about Luther Johns?”

“He ain’t so important.”

“Don’t be too plumb certain. Bet a hat you’ll find he’s plenty enough important. Now keep yore shirt on, Tom, an’ go dance with that little heifer in the red dress. Have a good time. Watch me step this with that tall señorita in green.”

DEATH TRAILS

IT WAS DAWN WHEN Ike Babcock beckoned to Tom Stroud. As Tom joined the big cattleman, Ike said:

"Let's go over an' visit the Cayuse Cattle Pool, Tom."

Again they stood outside the window, against the wall. Ike called out in a soft drawl: "How's she a-payin' inside?"

Luther Johns was at the bars of the window, snarling, screaming, cursing, begging.

"Let me out, Babcock. Take all I have. But let me out!"

"You'll be out, directly, Luther. Git back from that window. It's Kid Brady I want to talk with. Knock Johns away from that window, Kid."

From inside, the voice of Kid Brady, flat, toneless: "Stand away from the window, Johns, or I'll shoot you away from it. I got somethin' to tell Ike Babcock."

"I just got yore message, Kid, that you wanted more guns," said Ike when Kid Brady's face appeared at the bars. "How's tricks?"

"All aces, Ike."

"They talked?"

"Talked their heads off. I'm tired listenin'. I got it all for you, Ike."

"Anybody hurt in there?"

"Jackson's still sleepin'. So is Kennedy. I had to rap 'em hard. Like I figgered, they had 'er made to kill me. The big show come off just when it was daylight enough to see. Sounded like the battle o' Gettysburg when the three of 'em opened up on me."

"You hurt any, Kid?"

"Face got powder-burned when I closed in on 'em. Never had a better time in my life, Ike. There they was, bangin' away at me, wonderin' why I didn't drop. All three of 'em plumb snaky. All of 'em hog-wild when I told 'em my game. All bent on killin' me. And none of 'em knowin' that all they had in their guns was trick cartridges that wouldn't kill a pack rat. I got Kennedy an' Jackson tied up. I let Luther kind o' run loose because now an' then he charges me an' I kin knock him down. Yeah, it was a good show, Ike."

"Got all the information we need, then?"

"Enough to hang 'em all, Ike, and some left over. Luther's yore man."

"So I always figgered. I'll unlock the door, Kid. Git Luther's hands tied."

"What's the game?" asked Tom.

"You'll see, Tom. Luther Johns is goin' to write out what he knows. Then he'll git all the *marijuana* an' *tequila* he wants. Because when a man is goin' to die, he's 'titled to smokin' an' liquor an' good grub, an' I'm givin' Luther them things."

Ike Babcock unlocked the door. Kid Brady pushed Luther Johns outside. The man was a quivering, half-insane thing. His scarred face was ghastly, grayish, twitching. His one eye was a bloodshot, glazed slit. He shambled as he walked.

Kid Brady was no beautiful sight. One eye was black, swollen shut. There was a long gash on his forehead. His face was powder-burned, streaked with dried blood. His clothes were half torn off.

"I'd fight the rest o' Mexico, Ike, for some red pop an' a square meal. Got any gum on you?"

Ike handed over a package of gum, then closed the

cabin door, locking Kennedy and Jackson inside.

"I told you to holler if you needed he'p, Kid."

"I didn't need help, Ike. If it had come to a fight, I could 'a' killed 'em, couldn't I?"

"The Kid, here," Ike explained to Tom, "was the only man in there who had real ca'tridges in his gun. Well, let's git on to the house, boys. Git along, Luther. You got a smoke a-comin'."

Tom Stroud and Kid Brady kept hold of Luther Johns as they went to the house. Inside, Ike nodded to Kid Brady.

"Cut him loose, Kid." He put out a bottle of *tequila* and a box of *marijuana* cigarettes.

Kid Brady lighted the cigarette for the one-eyed renegade, for the man's hands shook so badly he could not hold a match.

Half an hour later Ike Babcock took away the *tequila* and doped cigarettes. He handed Luther Johns pen and ink and paper.

"Write 'er out, Luther. All of it. Then you kin have back yore cigarettes an' *tequila.* Git busy."

"I'm ready to die right now, Babcock. Go ahead and kill me if you want."

"Write all that you blabbed, there in the cabin. I've never killed a man without givin' him an even break. Write."

Ike reached into a drawer and pulled out two white-handled six-guns in their holsters. The loops of the belt were filled. He laid the guns and belt on the table.

"Real ca'tridges in 'em, Luther. You'll git yore chance to reach Cayuse. Write 'er out."

Kid Brady was already on his third bottle of red pop. He handed Tom a bottle.

"It beats hard liquor, Tom."

"I'll take yore word for it, Kid."

Ike sat in his big chair, watching Luther Johns write. For half an hour, no man spoke. Luther Johns kept writing. Twice, Ike poured the man a stiff drink to steady his nerves.

Finally, Luther Johns laid aside his pen. He stood up, looking more than ever like a buzzard.

"There it is, Babcock. Read it. It's my death warrant. It has my signature at the bottom. Give me those cigarettes and the bottle. Then kill me if you like."

"Give him his smokes an' liquor, Kid," said Ike Babcock, as he read the document.

Ike Babcock folded the signed document and put it in his pocket. Then he handed Luther his belt and guns.

"You'll have an hour's start, Luther. You'll be ridin' a good horse. Nobody will stop you. Take along what you need in the way o' hop an' liquor. You'll need a brave maker. You told me one time that you wasn't scared o' any man. I'm givin' you yore chance to prove it. If you ain't rabbit-hearted, you'll wait for me at Smoke Signal Pass. I'll have this document. Now git out. I'm killin' you on sight."

Luther Johns pocketed the cigarettes and bottle and buckled on his guns.

"I'll wait, Babcock."

"I'll have this paper on me, Luther. If you kill me, it's yourn to destroy. Nobody will see it but me."

"That's fair, Babcock. Better than I deserve. But that won't keep me from killing you if I can."

"One thing before yuh go, Luther. Make out an I O U to Tom Stroud for one hundred dollars."

"What for?"

"Tom give you four hundred, there in Cayuse. One hundred apiece to bury you an' Kennedy an' Jackson an' Kid Brady."

Luther Johns, himself once more, smiled sardonically. "Why does he get the hundred back?"

"You ain't havin' no hundred-dollar funeral, that's why. I'm plantin' you like I'd bury a dead skunk, there at Smoke Signal Pass. Make 'er out."

"Make 'er out for two hundred," put in Kid Brady, "because Tom Stroud ain't goin' to kill me. Ike knows he won't, don't you, Ike? Will Tom kill me?"

"Make 'er two hundred," said Ike.

Luther Johns took pen and paper once more. He made out the I 0 U and tossed it across the table to Tom Stroud. Then he settled his gun belt down across his bony hips.

"I'll be waiting at Smoke Signal Pass, Babcock."

Luther Johns had gone. The chapel bells were calling the faithful to Mass. The sun was rising. Ike Babcock turned to Kid Brady.

"Fetch Jackson here."

Five minutes later, Jackson, his face mask-like, his eyes cold, deadly, stood in the room.

"You git an hour's start, Jackson, and take yore chances, or you kin go back acrost the border under guard to be tried for the murder o' Tom Stroud's younger brother, one night at Cayuse. The kid you murdered, Jackson."

"I'll take my head start, Babcock. Or I'll shoot it out with Tom Stroud here an' now."

"I'll just call that," snapped Tom.

"You ain't callin' nobody, Tom," said Ike. "You just set back an' let me handle the reins. Jackson, you want that head start?"

"All I'm askin' for is a gun and a horse. I'll play my string out, Babcock. I got nothin' to lose."

"Give Jackson an hour,. Tom. Then ride him down and kill him. Here's yore gun Jackson. There's a horse at the barn. Tom Stroud, Texas Ranger, is goin' to ketch up with you somewheres."

"And when I do," said Tom, "I'm squarin' a debt."

"When you do, Stroud, I'll pay off one, myself. Yore father sent me to the pen once. I paid off a little of it when I got that brother o' yours. Now I'll finish payin' off, Mr. Ranger."

"The trail north is blocked, Jackson," said Ike Babcock. "That eastward trail is open. Take it. Tom will ketch up with you because he'll be ridin' a better horse. You got an hour's start. Take it. Git out. Here's a quart to take along. It'll be yore last, so drink hearty on the way."

Jackson glared at Tom. "I'll be glad to meet you again, Stroud."

"That goes double, Jackson. And I'm givin' you the advantage o' the rocks to hide behind."

"I don't need no ambush for you, Ranger." Jackson went out the door.

"Fetch in Kennedy, Kid," said Ike Babcock. "Tom, set down. Chaw on the Kid's gum."

King Kennedy was brought in. His face was mottled, flabby, and his pale eyes were staring widely.

"Gimme a drink, Babcock."

"He'p yorese'f, King. Drink all you want. Kid, fetch in Cassidy an' the Chick feller. Kennedy, them border patrol men is takin' you outta Mexico. Takin' you back to be tried for murder. Luther's gone up the trail through Smoke Signal Pass. Jackson's headed acrost the east trail. When you git yore stomach full o' liquor an' grub, Cassidy an' Chick will take you acrost by the old Farias place. With you goes the three sons Farias left behind when he died. Drink hearty, Kennedy. Fill that fat paunch o' yourn for the last time. Because if you ain't dead when you cross the border, you'll be hung pronto. Eh, Kid?"

Kid Brady, with Cassidy and Chick, had just come in.

"What was it you said, Ike?"

"I said, Kid, that you better git King Kennedy his gun—He'll have his chance, the same as Luther an' Jackson. Give Cassidy an' Chick their guns. Cassidy, you'll take King Kennedy to Cayuse an' hold him on a murder charge. Watch him, an' don't give him a chance to shoot you in the back. I'm sendin' along three Mexican vaqueros who know the trail. Till you reach the border, yo're under their orders. Got that straight, both of you?"

"Why are we taking Kennedy?" asked Cassidy.

"Because there's an order signed for his arrest. The warrant reads dead or alive. It's signed by authorities on both sides o' the border. Here it is. Keep it."

Kennedy's thick hand shook as he lifted his drink. He set down the empty glass.

"Babcock, this is murder! You know it's murder!"

"Cassidy," said Ike Babcock, ignoring Kennedy's plea, "here is the warrant. It's signed and stamped with the seals of the United States and the Republic of Mexico. Take yore prisoner. Let him keep his gun. Hope you have a good trip up the trail."

"What about you, Stroud?" asked Cassidy.

"I'd take Ike Babcock's advice, Cassidy, if I was you."

"What's become of Luther Johns and Jackson?" asked Chick.

"They're headed for home," said Tom Stroud. "They'll be took care of."

"You're not coming with us, Stroud?" asked Cassidy.
"No. I'll go along another trail. I'll meet you in Cayuse, if my luck is good."

END OF THE CATTLE POOL

FOR FIVE MILES TOM Stroud followed the trail that led eastward. Then he pulled up, a worried look on his face. He had been watching the trail for sign. At the creek crossing, down through a sand wash, not a shod track, no track of any kind, marked the trail. Jackson had not come that way. Jackson had taken another trail.

Tom whirled his horse and headed back for the ranch. He rode hard, and as he rode, he tried to puzzle it out. What trail had Jackson taken? What had made him change his plans? Nor fear, because Jackson was no coward.

At the barn, when he reached the ranch, Torn found a bunch of cowboys shooting craps.

"Back so quick, Tom?" said a grizzled Texan. "Thought you was gone to Cayuse?"

"Listen, pardner, I want the truth outta you boys or I'll pound it outta somebody with a gun barrel. What trail did Jackson take?"

"He taken the Smoke Signal Pass trail, Tom. Now don't git huffy. Tuck in yore shirt. Ike's orders was to send Luther Johns and Jackson up the Smoke Signal Pass trail. Don't git ringy at us, feller. We hazed Luther up that direction. Half an hour later we sends Jackson along with our best regards."

"Who follered 'em?" asked Tom.

"Ike and Kid Brady. Ike said that if you showed up, to have you wait till he got back."

"What Ike said ain't stoppin' me."

Tom was off at a long lope. The cowboys looked at one another, but no man tried to stop Tom.

Tom pushed his horse to the limit. He saw it all now. Ike had tricked him. Big Ike Babcock aimed to trail Luther Johns and Jackson and kill them.

The going was slow as Tom followed the twisting trail up across the mountains. Seconds seemed hours. He wanted to take Jackson alive. He wanted to take him across the border and throw him in jail. He'd planned to cripple Jackson's gun arm with a bullet and take him alive. But Ike had outfoxed him. Made a fool of him.

Now he was nearing the pass. He heard the crunch of gravel under shod hoof, the breaking of brush. Somebody was coming down the trail. Now, whover it was, had left the trail and dodged into the brush. The rider must have sighted Tom and quit the main trail.

Tom Stroud eased his horse off the trail and dismounted. He had no intention of riding into an ambush. If that was Jackson or Luther Johns, they would be laying for him. Tom unbuckled his chaps and threw them across his saddle. He took off his spurs. Then, his six-gun in his hand, he started cautiously up the mountainside, keeping off the trail.

A horse nickered up there in the manzanita thicket. Tom heard his horse give answer. He saw a nest of granite boulders. If he could only make the boulders, he'd be able to put up a fight. He started to wriggle his way through some light brush. The man above opened up. A stabbing, burning pain caught Tom's right arm. The man's next shot tore through his hat as he rolled back into the thick brush below. Bullets snarled around him.

From up ahead in the pass came the sound of shots.

Tom jerked off his neck scarf and twisted a tourniquet above his broken arm. The bullet had smashed the bone below the elbow.

The shot had loosened Tom's hold on his gun. The weapon had dropped out of his hand and rolled down the slope. It was lost somewhere in the brush. He swore under his breath as he jerked the tourniquet tight with his left hand and his teeth. Unarmed now, he was at the mercy of the man up there on the trail. Jackson, perhaps, or Luther Johns.

He had seen his gun roll down the slope. Even under normal conditions it would take no little time to find it. And to search for it, there in the sparse undergrowth, meant making a target of himself.

The shooting had scared his horse. He saw the big bay gelding going down the trail, head held sidewise, to keep from stepping on the dragging bridle reins. He was afoot. His arm broken. Without a gun.

The man above him had ceased firing. Tom put his hat on a stick and lifted it slowly. Immediately a shot ripped out, and Tom let the hat drop. He rolled to one side as more bullets pounded into the dirt where he had been lying. Whoever was doing that shooting was no slouch with a gun.

"If he'd run outta cartridges," muttered Tom, "I'd tackle him, whoever he is."

He remembered that Luther Johns had only twelve cartridges in his two guns. Jackson had half that number in his revolver. Tom poked his hat into sight once more. But no shots came his way. Either the man was on to the trick or he was low on cartridges.

Tom's arm was commencing to throb with pain. The shooting up there in the pass had stopped.

Maybe some of Ike's men would come up the trail.

Not likely, though. They were under Ike's orders to stay there and protect the ranch in case of an attack from the troops that were coming up from the south.

Nothing to do but play a waiting game. What had happened to Ike and Kid Brady? Was it Jackson, up there behind that brush, or was it Luther Johns?

Tom crawled slowly to the edge of the brush. Then he almost cried out aloud with joy. There, in a bare space where the brush was thin, he saw the glitter of blued steel. His gun!

He twisted the neck scarf tighter around his right arm. He was not much of a shot with his left hand, but he'd make a stab at trying to hit his mark. First job was to get that gun.

He crouched there in the brush, his eyes measuring every inch of the rough ground that lay between him and his gun. The distance was probably twenty feet. Downhill and the slant was steep. Then another ten feet after he'd got the gun, to some rocks.

One chance in a hundred. One in a thousand, judging from the way that hombre was shooting. But taking that chance would beat being bushed up like a coyote.

Tom shifted to a crouching position, like a foot racer at the starting mark. His jaws were clamped tight. He forgot the pain of his shattered arm. His goal was that bit of blued steel that glittered in the sunlight.

"Here goes nothin'!"

Split seconds. The crack of gunfire. Tom lost his footing, rolled over, dived for the gun. A bullet threw dirt in his face. Pain tore through his arm as his fall threw his weight on the broken bone. Now he had his gun. He was back on his feet, crouched, running, stumbling. Then shelter. And even as he gained shelter, he jerked the trigger of his gun. The man above him, a big, bulky form, lost his balance and came rolling down the slope. Tom was on top of him, clubbing at the other man's gun hand. He smashed the gun from the man's hand and ground his face in the dirt.

Tom Stroud, dazed, his senses dulled by pain and excitement, did not see the man up on the trail who stood there, a smoking six-gun in his hand. Not until the man called out.

"I'd say, Tom, that the fight belonged to you!"

Tom's head jerked up. He saw Kid Brady shoving his gun back in its holster.

"Best show I've seen in a coon's age, Tom. It's over now. King Kennedy ain't botherin' nobody no more."

"Kennedy!" Tom, who had been astride the big man, got to his feet. He turned the limp form over and looked into the mottled face of King Kennedy.

Kennedy's pale eyes were slitted. His face was pain-twisted, horrible. Kid Brady walked down the slope, his spurs jingling. He looked down into Kennedy's eyes. Tom, dizzy with pain, stood by.

"Got anything to say, Kennedy?" asked Kid Brady.

"Only this, Kid. I'll see you in hell some day. We'll take it up there."

"Suits me, Kennedy. I want you to know this much before you die. I always hated you. The money you paid me I give away because it was too dirty even for Kid Brady. I had a dad once who got in yore way. You killed him. You and Jackson and Luther Johns. Ike Babcock picked me up. I was about ten years old then. You got paid off, Kennedy. I'll go where you go, I reckon, but I ain't scared to go. Yo're scared, Kennedy. Scared. Look at his eyes, Tom. See the scared look in 'em? So long, you dirty, murderin' son."

Tom looked down at the big man's face. It was

stamped with fear.

"He's dead, Tom."

"I had to kill him," muttered Tom. "I didn't want to kill him. But he was shootin' at me."

Kid Brady ejected an empty shell from his six-gun. He grinned.

"You missed him a mile, Tom. But you nearly got me. I killed King Kennedy."

"You got 'im, Kid?"

Kid Brady shoved a cartridge into the empty chamber of his gun, then held out his hand.

"Mebbeso we'll meet up again some day, Tom. Don't bear me no grudge, pardner. Go set down on the trail. Ike will be down directly. He's fetchin' along Jackson." Kid Brady gripped Tom's left hand. "Hope we meet again, Tom."

Tom Stroud watched Kid Brady scramble up the slope. A few moments later he saw the Kid ride down the trail at a reckless speed.

Tom had hardly reached the trail when Ike Babcock showed up. Ike had an ugly bullet wound through his cheek. But he grinned through the crude bandage.

"Just turned Jackson over to Cassidy, Tom. Cassidy an' Chick is takin' him to Cayuse. Hurt bad?"

"Just a busted arm, Ike."

"My horse will pack double. You git in the saddle. I'll ride behind."

"Just a minute, Ike. Kennedy is—"

"Is dead. I seen the whole play, son. And Kid Brady has drifted yonderly for a spell until everything gits quiet. Climb aboard the southbound express."

Ike helped him mount, then got on behind. He took a flask from his pocket and made Tom drink. Ike's big gelding took them down the trail.

"Tom, I knowed that Kennedy would make a break. I kinda figgered that a way. He got his chance, there at the old Farias ranch. Seems like Cassidy an' Chick was hampered some by them Mexican boys I sent along. Then Kennedy outfoxed the Mexicans an' started to make 'er through the pass while me an' the Kid was ketchin' Jackson an' Luther Johns. The shootin' stampeded him down the trail. I didn't figger on you comin' up the trail. Well, Kennedy ain't a king no more. How's the arm?"

"It's all right, Ike. But how about Luther Johns?"

"Luther," said Ike, "went the same trail Kennedy taken. That writin' he did at the house is a complete confession sayin' how he killed yore dad, down in Texas."

"Luther Johns killed my dad?"

"And yore dad was my best friend. I done squared the debt, Tom. It was my job."

They rode on in silence for some time. Then Ike began talking through the bloodstained bandage across his mouth.

"The Cayuse Cattle Pool ain't no more, Tom. That nest o' rattlesnakes is gone. Jackson will hang. As fer me, Tom, I've done some bad things, and I'm ashamed fer it. But I've not hurt anyone in the doin'. Anyway, I'm through with all that. I'm goin' t' stay right here in Mexico and run my ranch all legal and proper like, and in time I'll be able to give back all the cattle I've 'borrowed.' "

"Ike, when my kid brother worked for you, did you know who he was? What he was after?"

"Not till it was too late to keep Jackson from murderin' him, Tom. It was him that told you I never killed yore dad, wasn't it?"

"Yes. He wrote me a letter sayin' he'd run on to the men that had framed the deal. He didn't say who the killer was. But he sent for me to come to Cayuse. I got there too late, Ike. But how did you know he wrote me? Did he tell you?"

"The letter was in his pocket when Jackson killed him. Kid Brady got it outta the boy's pocket and give it to me. I sent it on to you."

"Then you knowed all along?"

"Yeah. I knowed all along, Tom. And now, we kin really git acquainted. I want you to stay down here with me. Kind of a pardner. I need you."

"Gosh, Ike, I—"

"No excuses goes. You stay. I hired you once as ramrod, and when I hire a man, he's done hired."

"Ike, I can't tell you how I feel. I feel—"

"You'll feel better when we git to the ranch. Doggone, now, don't it make you sick to think we're both bunged up an' the *muy grande fiesta* comin' up?"

"What *muy grande fiesta?*" For the first time in the past few hours Tom recalled the fact that Ruiz and Ike expected a battle with the federal troops.

"Didn't they tell you at the ranch? Them troops was just the *presidente's* military escort. I got the news just before I started after Luther Johns an' Jackson. I been pullin' strings for a year or more to git Colonel Ruiz made governor o' this State. I done cut the mustard. Ruiz is the new governor. And we're goin' to pull off the biggest fiesta you ever seen. Say, I bet you a hat he'd be governor. I'll pick me out the best I kin buy. Now git this geldin' along, son. You an' me is agoin' home."

We hope that you enjoyed reading this
Sagebrush Large Print Western.
If you would like to read more Sagebrush titles,
ask your librarian or contact the Publishers:

United States and Canada

Thomas T. Beeler, *Publisher*
Post Office Box 659
Hampton Falls, New Hampshire 03844-0659
(800) 818-7574

**United Kingdom, Eire, and
the Republic of South Africa**

Isis Publishing Ltd
7 Centremead
Osney Mead
Oxford OX2 0ES England
(01865) 250333

Australia and New Zealand

Bolinda Publishing Pty. Ltd.
17 Mohr Street
Tullamarine, 3043, Victoria, Australia
(016103) 9338 0666